Return to Dunquin Cove

By

Rodney Riesel

Published by Island Holiday Publishing
East Greenbush, NY

ISBN: 978-0-9894877-7-1
First Edition

Special thanks to:
Pamela Guerriere
Kevin Cook

Cover Design by:
Connie Fitsik

To obtain more copies of this book friend me at

https://www.facebook.com/rodneyriesel

For Brenda
Kayleigh, Ethan,
&
Peyton

Chapter One

It was Wednesday morning, and Ben Dunning could hear the birds chirping outside the bedroom window before he even opened his eyes. He felt around the mattress for his pillow, found it, and dragged it across the bed and up over his head. The pillow blocked out most of the morning sunlight but didn't seem to muffle the birds at all.

He rolled over onto his back and stared up at the crack in the ceiling that he'd been meaning to fix for months now. He rubbed his eyes with his fingertips and raised his head to look toward the windows. The light shining through was bright and he squinted a little. *Why does she have to open those blinds so damn early in the morning?* he thought. He let his head drop back onto the mattress.

As Claire walked into the bedroom, she was humming one of those made-up melodies that people sometimes hum while doing housework. "Getting up, sleepyhead?" she asked.

Ben let out a groan.

Claire set a laundry basket on the floor, then opened the top dresser drawer and began filling it with folded socks, underwear, and t-shirts. "Maybe you're too old to stay out so late playing cards with the big boys."

Ben rolled to his side and watched Claire as she put away the clothes. Every time she bent over to take something out of the basket, the black T-shirt she was wearing rode up just enough to see a few inches of her butt cheeks. Ben liked what he saw. "Not too old to play cards, but definitely too old to drink that damn moonshine Curt makes," he said, referring to Curt Holliday, one of the many friends he had made since arriving in Dunquin Cove, Maine.

"Well, if you can't run with the big dogs you better stay on the porch," Claire joked. She bent over one last time to grab the last pair of socks from the basket. She looked back at Ben, who was wearing a devilish grin. "What are you smiling about?"

"Just enjoying the show."

Claire pulled at the bottom of the T-shirt. "Perv."

"Maybe you should climb back in here," Ben suggested.

Claire put her hands on her hips. "Maybe you should just get up."

"Oh, I'm up."

Claire turned and walked to the bedroom door, looking at Mica's door to make sure it was still closed. She quietly pushed her own door closed and turned the lock. When she turned around, Ben was holding the blankets open. She pulled her T-shirt up over her head and let it drop to the floor.

Ben's eyes bugged out like a cartoon wolf. "Ah-OOO-gah!"

Claire ran to the bed and jumped in. "We need to be quiet or Mica will hear us."

"Tell that to these squeaky old bed springs."

"Just try to hold it down, okay?"

"Okay. Permission to come aboard, captain."

"Granted … ooooh! On second thought, sailor, make all the noise you want."

Chapter Two

"Mica! Come on, you're breakfast is getting cold!" Claire hollered up the stairs. Mica said nothing. "Mica!"

"I'm coming!"

Ben sat at the dining room table flipping through the pages of the *Dunquin Crier.* He glanced across the table at Mica's untouched breakfast plate and then shoved the last of his own scrambled eggs into his mouth.

Claire walked back down the hallway, through the dining room, and into the kitchen. "He's going to miss the bus if he doesn't get moving," she griped as she passed through.

Seconds later, Ben lifted his head from the paper when he heard the school bus come to a stop in front of The Colsome House Bed and Breakfast. He pushed his chair back, got up, and made his way toward the front door. He opened the door and then looked up the staircase. There was no sign of Mica. Ben pushed open the screen and waved the bus on. The bus driver waved back, put the bus in gear, and sped off to the next stop.

Mica ran down the stairs. "Was that the school bus?" he asked.

"Yes," Ben answered. "Your breakfast is on the table. Give me a few minutes to get dressed and I'll take you to school."

"Thanks, Ben," Mica blurted out as he ran down the hall.

Ben slowly shook his head as he made his way up the stairs. Being a father figure was still pretty new to Ben and even though he didn't have children of his own, it was a roll he was happily settling into even more rapidly than he had expected.

It had been almost six months since the morning Ben had stumbled into the front yard of Claire's B&B, as she raked up the fallen leaves. He had just been involved in an auto accident and didn't know who, or where he was. Claire spent two days nursing Ben back to health as he lay in the bed in room number four.

Ben had now become part of the family; a father figure to Mica, and a partner and lover to Claire.

Ben had never fully regained the memories of his past. As far as the citizens of Dunquin Cove were concerned, he was Ben Dunning, Claire's brother-in-law, the brother of her deceased husband Clay, who had passed away three years earlier. It was a story that Ben and Claire had created on the fly, one morning and it stuck.

*****

A few minutes later Ben returned to the dining room, dressed in jeans and a dark gray, long-sleeved T-shirt. "You ready?"

The ten year old crammed the last of his toast into his mouth with a muffled, "Yup."

Ben pushed the sleeves of his shirt up to his elbows and grabbed the van keys off of the buffet as he walked by. "Come on, pal."

Mica jumped up from the table, grabbed his backpack that hung on the chair behind him, and followed Ben out the back door.

The minivan was parked in the driveway in front of the garage door, facing toward the street. Ben and Mica both stopped dead in their tracks when they noticed the flat front tire. "Shit!" Ben remarked. "Uh, sorry, Mica. Let's keep the cussing between you and me."

"Okay. How am I going to get to school now?"

"Only one thing we can do. We'll change the tire, and you'll just have to be a little late for school."

Mica turned and headed toward the back door. "Good, I have math first period."

"Where are you going?"

"Back in the house."

"Aren't you going to help me change the tire?"

Mica let out a sigh. "I guess so."

"Don't sound so excited," Ben shot back sarcastically.

Mica removed his backpack, opened the van door, and set it on the passenger seat.

"Pop the back hatch," Ben called out as he made his way around the back of the vehicle.

Mica reached across the steering wheel and pressed the button. The hatch opened.

Ben removed the jack and the spare and carried them to the front of the van. He leaned the tire against the door and knelt down to slide the jack underneath the frame of the van. When he had finished jacking it up, he inspected the tire as he turned it. Not finding a hole or any other obvious reason for the tire to be flat, he concluded, "Your mother must have hit a curb. Maybe Artie can patch it."

"She'll never admit to it," Mica said, handing Ben the tire iron.

"That's why we won't even mention it."

Mica chuckled. "Good idea."

They had just finished installing the spare when the back screen door creaked open. Ben and Mica looked at each other.

"What's the matter?" Claire called out from the doorway.

"Flat tire," Mica responded.

"Huh. How did that happen?"

"Can't imagine," Ben answered.

"Must have run over a nail."

Ben tightened the lug nuts. "Must have been."

Claire let the screen door shut and went back into the house.

Ben smacked the plastic hubcap with the palm of his hand, snapping it back into place. "Turn that jack handle counter-clockwise."

Mica took hold of the jack handle and began spinning it; the van slowly lowered.

Ben rolled the flat tire to the back of the van and set it inside. Mica lay the jack and handle next to the tire, then grabbed the tire iron and tossed it in. Ben closed the hatch.

Mica looked at his grimy paws. "Better wash my hands."

"Yeah, me too," Ben agreed, and they headed for the door.

"How do you know when to lie and when to tell the truth?"

Ben stopped, turned, and put his hand on Mica's shoulder. "What do you mean?"

"You lied to my mom and told her it was probably a nail."

"That wasn't really a lie."

"It wasn't the truth."

"Right."

"If you're not telling the truth, aren't you lying?"

"Not always."

"What's the difference?"

Ben thought for a second. "Sometimes there's a gray area between a lie and the truth."

"Huh. What's that called?"

"That's called the *you can't win* area."

"How will I know when something falls in the *you can't win* area?"

Ben mussed Mica's rust colored mop of hair. "You'll know, pal, you'll know."

Chapter Three

After Ben dropped Mica off at school he did a U-turn and headed back down Maple Avenue. He took a left onto Main Street, drove down two blocks, and pulled into Lenny's Auto Repair. The window was down on the minivan and Ben could hear the *ding* as he drove over the thin black hose that ran on the ground across the driveway. *No sneaking up on Artie*, he thought.

Ben brought the van to a stop in front of one of the two garage doors, shut off the engine, and pressed the button to open the back hatch. When he climbed out of the van, he looked around for Artie.

Parked next to the garage was a red and white 1994 Ford F-150 with an extended cab and seven foot bed. Sticking out from underneath the truck were Artie's legs. He was lying on a mechanic's dolly, and he rolled himself out from underneath the truck as Ben approached.

"Mornin'," Artie said.

"Mornin'," Ben returned. "Whatcha got going on under there?"

"Just gotta change the oil and then slap a for-sale sign on her."

"How much?"

"Thirty-five hundred."

Ben walked back to his van and Artie followed.

"How many miles on her?"

"Hundred and fifty thousand."

Artie peered into the back of the van. "Looks like you got yourself a flat tire there, Ben."

"I was wondering why the air wouldn't stay on the inside," Ben said quipped. "You're one hell of a mechanic, Artie."

"And you're as full of shit as a Christmas turkey," Artie said good-naturedly. He stuck his thumbs in his suspenders, ran them up and down a few times, and leaned back on his heels. "Won't be able to patch her, though. Looks like there's a puncture right there in the sidewall."

Ben looked doubtful. "Are you sure? I couldn't find a hole anywhere."

"You couldn't? aw, poor Claire," joked Artie, grinning. He hauled out the tire and pointed. "See, it's right here."

"Huh. Have you got a new tire you can put on the rim?" Ben asked.

"I can sure check for you."

Ben followed Artie, who was carrying the tire, in through one of the overhead doors to the back of the building, where several new and used tires sat on a steel rack. Artie squinted as he looked down through his inventory. "Ain't got one," he said. Then Ben followed him into the office. "Help yourself to a cup of coffee there, Ben. Just made it fresh yesterday."

Ben looked over at the old crusty coffee maker that sat, with a few stained cups and a half-eaten box of donuts, on a table under the flyspecked front window. "Thanks, but I think I'll pass."

Humming off key, Artie flipped through the Goodyear catalog until he found what he was looking for. "There," he said, tapping the page with his greasy finger. "I can have you one here tomorrow morning. Hundred and seventy-nine dollars including, mounting and balance."

"Sounds good, Artie, go ahead and order it."

"You got it."

Ben left the service station and took a left onto Shore Drive and then a left onto Denton Street. He pulled to the curb in front of Cargill Hardware. Maude Everly was standing on the sidewalk in front of the store moving in a small circle as she swept pieces of broken plastic into a small pile. Ben glanced up at the broken sign that hung over the door as he climbed from the van.

"Damn kids," Maude commented.

"When did this happen?" Ben asked.

"Sometime last night."

Ben bent down, grabbed the dustpan that lay at Maude's feet, and held it for her as she swept the bits of plastic into it. "You have a security camera?" he asked.

Maude pointed at a small black camera mounted on the wall behind her. "Right there."

"That's good."

"It would be good, *if* it was hooked up. Mr. Cargill installed the cameras himself. Hooked up the three inside the store but never did the one outside. Said it didn't need to be hooked up. Said just having the camera there would deter anyone from doing anything illegal."

"Guess he was wrong." Carrying the dustpan, Ben followed Maude into the store.

"Here, I can take that," Maude said. She took the sweepings from Ben and dumped them into the trashcan behind the checkout counter. "What can I do for you today, Ben?"

Ben pulled a small piece of paper from his back pocket. "I need you to mix some paint for me."

Maude grabbed a pen and slid a pad of paper in front of her. "Shoot."

"Six gallons of Bavarian Cream, flat, two gallons of Dragon Fly, satin, one gallon of Twilight Gold, semi-gloss, and one gallon of Lewd Sorbet, also semi-gloss."

"All exterior, I take it."

"Yup." Ben put the list back in his pocket.

"Is that gonna be enough for that big old bed and breakfast?"

"It'll be a start."

Maude slid the pad back over next to the register. "Okay, you can pick it up later this afternoon."

"Thanks, Maude." As he exited, he wondered if he had bitten off more that he could chew. As far as he knew, he had never painted a house in his life, and the B&B, being such a large and ornate old Victorian, was sure to be challenge.

Chapter Four

Ben lifted the twenty-four-foot wooden extension ladder off of the three twenty-penny nails from which it hung on the garage wall. He carried it around to the front yard, leaned it against the house, and pulled the rope to extend it. *Snap!*

"Dammit!" Ben cursed as he watched the other end of the rope slide through the pulley and hit the ground next to him. He dropped the end of rope he was holding, grabbed one of the rungs, and shoved it upwards, extending the ladder manually. When he reached the height he wanted he leaned the ladder back against the house and moved the legs around until he found a level spot.

Returning to the garage, he found a paint scraper, a wire brush, and a chisel. He put the scraper and chisel in his back pocket and carried the wire brush back to the ladder.

As Ben began climbing the ladder, the third rung snapped, sending him sprawling to the ground on his back with a juicy-sounding *whoomph*. The impact knocked the wind out of him, and he gasped for air. He rolled to his side and removed the chisel and scraper from his back pocket and rubbed his aching ass. He let out a groan as he rolled over onto his knees and got up.

Standing in the doorway, Claire had seen the whole thing and tried not to laugh. "Are you okay?" she asked.

Ben dusted off his pants. "I'm fine."

"That ladder's pretty old," Claire said, stating the obvious.

Ben shot her a look and cocked his head. "Ya think?"

"You want me to call and see if you can borrow Marv's ladder?"

Ben looked over at his neighbor's house, a once majestic old Victorian in dire need of tender loving care. "No."

"I'm sure he wouldn't mind."

"I know he wouldn't mind. He would love to hear how I fell on my ass, and then he would help me carry the ladder over. Then he would tell me how to take care of a wooden ladder so that something like this wouldn't happen. Then he would stand here all day and watch me scrape and paint the house, telling me everything I was doing wrong."

"Oh, come on, he's not *that* bad. He's just old … and bored. Go over and get the ladder."

"Okay, okay," Ben said as he begrudgingly made his way next door to Marvin Polinowski's house.

Ben rapped on Marvin's door five times as loud as he could, knowing there was a good chance Marvin wouldn't hear him anyway. He waited for a few seconds and repeated his knock, and then he pushed the doorbell button.

Finally, Ben heard Marvin's rusty gate of a voice from within. "Keep your pants on; keep your pants on for Chrissakes! I told you I wasn't interested! Can't a guy take a shit around here without someone banging on his front door?"

Good God. Ben was already regretting his decision to ask to borrow the ladder. He heard Marvin sliding the security chain from its channel and disengaging the deadbolt before the doorknob finally turned.

The door creaked open and Ben instantly smelled old man—an earthy mix of weapons-grade BO and at least a gallon of Old Spice—a lethal assault on the nose.

"Oh, it's you … I was taking a shit," Marvin said.

"I heard," Ben responded.

"Who told you?"

"You."

"When?"

Ben changed the subject. "Can I borrow your ladder, Marvin?"

"Neither a borrower nor a lender be, for loan oft loses itself and friend—William Shakespeare," Marvin replied.

Ben stared at Marvin for a moment. "So … is that a no?"

Marvin shook his head. "I don't care if you borrow my goddamn ladder. It's an old ladder, and we're not friends anyway."

"Uh, okay, thanks. Is it in your garage?"

"It is. Let me put my shoes on, and I'll help you carry it over."

"You don't have to do that, Marvin."

"I know I don't *have* to do it, but if I don't, you'll probably knock something off the wall of the garage and break it." Marvin pulled the door open further. "Come on in, you can wait while I get my shoes on."

Ben followed Marvin into the living room and stood quietly while the old man squatted on the edge of a vintage Barcalounger and laboriously put on his shoes. This was the first time Ben had ever entered the Polinowski residence. The home had virtually the same floor plan as the bed and breakfast, and Ben figured the same carpenter had probably built it long ago. Unlike Claire's place, though, all of the floors were carpeted with shag carpeting and all of the moldings had been painted white. There were many framed photographs sitting on the mantle over the fireplace.

"You have children, Marvin?" Ben asked, trying to end the uncomfortable silence.

Marvin glanced up at the photographs. "Of course I have children!" he snapped back. "Why do you ask?"

Ben shrugged his shoulders. "I don't know." He motioned toward the mantle. "Just saw all of the pictures there."

Marvin tightened the Velcro straps on his sneakers, stood, and walked to the fireplace. He acted annoyed as he listed off his family members. "This here is my wife, Mary—been gone eleven years now." He pointed to the next picture. "This here is my boy, Jack__, enlisted in the Marines on his eighteenth birthday. Nine months later he was hit by a Jeep, walking from his tent to the mess tent. Sweet boy, but dumber than a sack of hammers.

Ben was wishing he hadn't mentioned the photos.

"These are my four girls, Theresa, Anna, Cara, and Virginia. Closest one lives up in Portland, one's in Florida, and the other two live out in Californy." Marvin stared at the pictures silently for a moment and then turned back to Ben. "Any other stupid questions, or can we get that ladder now?"

Ben said, "I think that's all for now."

Marvin walked down the hall, through the kitchen, and out the back door. Ben followed. Marvin had made it halfway to the garage when he stopped and turned back. "Hit that button right inside the back door."

Ben went back in and did as he was told; the garage door opened.

"Ladder's hanging right in here on the wall," Marvin said.

With Marvin's help, it took Ben twice as long as it should have to get the ladder around to the front of the house and up against the wall. "Thanks for your help, Marvin."

"Yup," Marvin responded. "Too cold to paint."

"The can says it has to be at least fifty-five degrees. Supposed to be sixty by noon."

"Weathermen have been known to be wrong," Marvin said disagreeably. He looked around. "Where's the paint?"

"Picking it up this afternoon. I was just going to scrape this morning."

"Got another scraper? I could show you how to do it the *right* way."

Ben got to the top of the ladder. "Nope, sorry. Just got the one."

"I'll look in my garage. I probably got one in there somewhere. I'll do the low parts."

Ben kept scraping.

"Whatcha doin' there, paintin'?" someone hollered.

Ben looked over his shoulder to see Alan Cobb crossing the street. He was in his usual get up: flannel shirt, jeans, white socks, and a pair of brown leather house moccasins. In his left hand he carried a rocks glass full of rum and Coke. In his early sixties, Cobb was a retired Air Force pilot and still sported a severe military buzz cut. He and his wife, Amy, had settled in Dunquin Cove right after he retired to be close to their daughter and son-in-law, who lived in York.

"Too cold to paint," Marvin hollered back. "He's just going to scrape this morning and pick up the paint this afternoon over to the hardware store."

"Got any more scrapers? We could give you a hand there, Ben," Cobb offered.

Ben shut his eyes for a few seconds and wished he__, or they__, were somewhere else. When he opened them again, his wish hadn't come true. "Just got the one," he replied calmly.

"I've probably got a couple in my garage," Marvin said.

Cobb took a sip of his drink. "How many paint brushes you got there, Ben?"

Oh my God. Ben pretended not to hear him and hoped the two men would eventually get bored and go home.

Marvin pointed at his garage. "I've got a bunch of old paint brushes in the garage__, we're covered."

We're. Ben cringed.

Cobb pulled a crumpled yellow door hanger from his back pocket. "You get one of these hanging on your doorknob yesterday, Marv?"

Marvin took the door hanger and looked at the front quickly, turned it over, and then handed it back to Cobb. "No. I made the mistake of answering the door, so I had one handed to me."

"You talk to them?"

"Nope. Took the paper they handed me and slammed the door in their face."

"What do you think it's about?"

"Don't know. Threw it in the garbage. Probably someone wants to tell us about our Lord and Savior."

Cobb folded the flier and stuffed it in his front pocket. "Naw, Marv, it says something about a new business, or something—some security outfit."

"Yeah, that's what they claim," said Marvin, his eyes gleaming. "I bet it's really one of them crazy religious cults, I bet! They suck you in, take all your money, and then mix up a big batch of Kool-Aid for everyone who wants to hitch a ride on their spaceship."

Ben rolled his eyes.

"You're probably right," Cobb agreed. "Well, I better head on back to the house and make me some lunch and another drink. Hey, Ben, I'll be back over later and give you a hand."

"You don't have to do that, Cobb," Ben shot back.

"Hey, what are neighbors for? Talk to you later, Marv." Cobb turned and made his way back across the street.

"Ben, I'm going to grab some lunch too," said Marvin. You going to be alright out here by yourself?"

"I think I'll be fine, Marv."

The old man scowled up at the sky. "Too cold to paint," he said, a little challenge in his tone.

Ben didn't take the bait.

Chapter Five

Ben closed the door behind him and stood in the foyer, closed his eyes tightly, and rubbed his temples.

"Looks like you had plenty of help out there for a while," Claire commented. "Did they all abandon you?"

Ben looked into the living room at Claire, who was sitting on the couch watching *Days of Our Lives*. "They'll be back," he said.

"Are you taking a break?"

"I just need some aspirins."

"I'll grab them for you." Claire stood. "It's not like I have anything else to do."

"Bored?" Ben asked.

"No guests, nothing to do."

"Any reservations?"

"Have a couple coming in Friday. I guess they're in town for a wedding."

"Well, I have an extra paint scraper."

"No thanks," Claire laughed. "I wouldn't want to cut in on your bonding time with Marv and Cobb."

Claire walked down the hall toward the kitchen, and Ben went into the living room and sat down. He noticed a stack of mail on the coffee table. Underneath the light bill was a postcard. Ben picked it up. On the front was a beach scene behind orange letters that read, GREETINGS FROM FORT LAUDERDALE. Ben smiled and turned the postcard over.

Ben & Claire,

Hope all is well. It's been a great six months in Florida. Just might move down here someday. We'll probably be in New Orleans by the time you get this. Miss you guys. Tell Mica we said hi.

Love,

Cam & Mildred

Ben tossed the postcard back on the table and thought about his friend Cam Owens for a second. He wondered if Cam knew how to paint a house. He knew Cam was good in a shootout, he saw that last spring, when Cam and his wife, Mildred stayed at the B&B. The elderly couple were two of three guests that were staying at the Colsome House when Ben staggered in that day.

"Came in the mail this morning," Claire said as she entered the room. She was holding the bottle of aspirin in one hand and a glass of water in the other.

"I kind of miss having those two around. I hope they come back through someday."

"Or maybe we could take a trip out to see them."

"Maybe."

Claire popped the top off of the aspirin bottle. "How many you want."

Ben leaned back on the couch and massaged his forehead. "Seventy-five."

"I'll give you three."

Claire handed the pills and glass to Ben. She bent to pick up the mail; a piece of yellow paper fell from the stack and landed on the floor at Ben's feet.

"What's this?" he said, picking it up.

"It was on the doorknob yesterday. I think they sell security systems or something."

"Oh, so that's what those old codgers were talking about." Ben read the door hanger.

PETRELLI & PERT
PRIVATE SECURITY
1-800-555-2321
OFFICES IN BOSTON,
PORTLAND,
AND SOON IN
DUNQUIN COVE
FEEL LESS THAN SAFE IN AN EVER-CHANGING
WORLD?
GIVE US A CALL!

Claire held out her hand and Ben gave her the hanger. "I feel safe," he joked.

"Me too." She bent and kissed him on the cheek. "Now that you're here."

Chapter Six

Ben pulled to the curb across the street from the hardware store. Parked directly in front of the store was a white van with red letters. HARBOR SIGNS, the letters read. *That was quick,* Ben thought.

"Looks like someone's getting a new sign," Claire said.

"Replacing the old one," Ben corrected. "Someone smashed it."

"Really? Who would do that?"

"Maude thinks it was some kids screwing around."

"Did she call the police?"

Ben and Claire climbed from the minivan. "I didn't ask."

One man stood on a six-foot step ladder as a second, younger, man did his best to lift the heavy plywood sign. Ben quickly went to the man's side and helped him lift.

The man on the ladder bent two metal straps around the pole and fastened a bolt and nut through each strap. After each nut had been tightened, the man on the ladder said, "There, that does it."

"Thanks, pal," the other man said.

"No problem," Ben answered.

The man on the ladder gave the sign a push and let it swing back and forth for a second to make sure it was going to stay put.

Claire went on into the hardware store. "Excuse me," she said as she walked between the men and the ladder.

Ben stepped back to get a look at the new sign. "Not quite as fancy as the old one," he commented.

The man on the ladder climbed down. "This one is just temporary. Old man Cargill just wanted something up there till the new one comes in. Probably be two weeks or so."

The man stuck out his hand. "Court Turner," he said.

Ben shook his hand. "Ben Dunning."

The younger man folded the stepladder and placed it in the back of the van.

"That there is my boy, Court Jr.," Court said.

Ben gave a nod to Junior; Junior nodded back.

"Dunning," Court repeated. "You have the B&B over on Shore Drive."

"I'm staying there. My sister-in-law owns it."

Court pulled a stack of business cards from his shirt pocket and handed one to Ben. "If you're ever in need of a new sign for the place, let me know."

Ben read the card and stuck it in his back pocket. "I'll sure do that, Court. Well I better get inside and pick up my paint."

"Is that what you do? Are you a painter, I mean?"

Ben thought for a second. "Um, yeah … I paint a little on the side."

"You got a business card on you?" Court asked.

"No. I ... um … I ran out of them a while back, and I haven't ordered any new ones."

"Oh, okay. Well, I'll catch you later." Court climbed in the passenger side of the van, his son started it up, and they drove away.

Ben pulled open the door of the hardware store and went in.

"Thinking about going into sign making?" Maude joked.

"No. I think I'm going to be a painter."

"A painter?" Claire asked.

"Yes. Why? You think I can't be a painter?"

"I think you can be a painter if you want to be a painter."

Ben picked up a cardboard box containing four gallons of paint. "Damn right I can."

"There's a hand truck over there," Maude said, pointing down one of the aisles.

Ben sat the box back down. "Good idea."

He wheeled the hand truck over and loaded the boxes of paint.

Maude ripped the top piece of paper off of her note pad. "Here," she said, handing it to Ben.

Ben looked at the name and number on the paper. "What's this?"

"A woman was in here this morning looking at paint samples. She asked if I knew anyone who did painting. Give her a call."

"Thank you, Maude," Ben said. He folded the paper and stuck it in his pocket, and then he gave Claire a big sarcastic smile. "See, I can be a painter if I want."

Claire walked to the door and held it open for him. "I hope this doesn't mean I have to pay you."

"I'll take it out in sex," Ben whispered as he pushed the cart past her.

Claire gave him a sly grin. "You promise?"

Chapter Seven

Alan Cobb had brought a lawn chair across the street and was sitting, drink in hand, facing the house. *The Dunquin Crier* lay folded on the ground next to his chair. He had brought it with him in case he became bored and wanted to read. Cobb was slumped down in the chair and had his legs stretched out in front of him, crossed at the ankles. "Looks like you missed a spot right up over the window there," he called out to Ben.

"I haven't gotten to that yet," Ben said calmly.

Cobb sipped his drink.

Marvin walked out of his front door and stood on the porch. He was smoking a cigar.

"Got another one of those?" Cobb yelled.

Marvin held up his wait-a-minute finger and went back inside, returning a few minutes later with another cigar.

"Here ya go," Marvin said, handing the stogie to Cobb.

"Thanks, neighbor."

Marvin walked over and grabbed one of Claire's chairs from her front porch and placed it next to Cobb's. "How's he doing?"

"I would have pressure-washed the house before I started scraping," Cobb said matter-of-factly. He rolled the tip of his cigar in his mouth to wet it, and then bit off the tip.

Marvin handed him his lighter. "Probably would have been a good idea."

Ben climbed down from the ladder and moved it to the other side of the window.

"Looks like you missed a spot right up over the window there," Marvin said, pointing his chicken bone of a finger at the spot.

Everyone's an expert. Ben took a deep breath. "I know. I'll get it." He climbed back up the ladder.

The front door opened and Claire stepped out onto the porch. Looking up at Ben she said, "I'm going to run and pick up Mica at school. Can I get you anything before I go?"

A gun, Ben thought. "No thanks," he said.

"A drink?" Claire offered.

Marvin spoke up. "I could use a drink."

"What can I get you, Marvin?"

"Whiskey and ginger ale, please."

"Sorry, Marvin—I have milk, Coke, and orange juice."

35

"Any vodka to go with that OJ," Marvin replied.

Cobb laughed.

"No, Marvin, I don't."

Cobb climbed out of his chair. "I'll make you a drink, Marv." He went back across the street and disappeared through his front door.

Claire returned her attention to Ben. "Did you want a soda?"

Ben started down the ladder. "No, but I think I'll ride along with you to pick up Mica."

"We'll be here when you get back, Ben," Marvin assured him.

"I'm going to leave the ladder up then, Marv."

"Yeah, you go ahead, I'll keep an eye on things here."

Claire held out the keys. "You want to drive?"

Ben waved her off. "No, I need to relax for a few minutes."

The two climbed in the van and headed down the street.

"Where's he going?" Cobb said and sat back down in his chair. He handed Marvin the drink he had made.

"Picking up the boy at school." Marvin took a sip of his drink.

"It takes both of them?"

"I guess."

Cobb sipped his drink. "He don't work very long before he takes a break."

"I noticed."

"People's work ethic just ain't the same as it was when we were his age."

"I had spent a year in Korea and two years in Vietnam before I was his age," Marvin commented. "*His* generation are a bunch of pussies."

"Hear! Hear!" Cobb held up his glass and Marvin did the same clinking them together. "To the *next* generation," Cobb said. "May they not be a bunch of pussies."

Marvin set his drink on the ground and groaned as he stood, walked over, and picked up one of the scrapers. "Come on, Cobb, grab that wire brush. This old house ain't gonna scrape itself."

Chapter Eight

Mica jumped in the van and slid the door closed.

"How was school today, pal?" Ben asked.

Mica fastened his seatbelt. "Okay."

"Just okay?"

"Yep."

"Learn anything new?"

"Yeah. Ramona McDuff kissed Billy Everly with her tongue."

Claire took a left onto Main Street. "I don't think that's what Ben meant by learn anything new."

Mica laughed. "I know."

"Billy Everly. Is he related to Maude over at the hardware store?" Ben asked.

"Maude is Billy's grandmother," Claire answered.

Ben turned around in his seat. "Mica, I'm going to go look at a painting job later. You want to go with me?"

Mica looked confused. "A painting job?"

Claire glanced up at her rearview mirror. "Ben's decided to become a professional painter."

Mica's eyes lit up. "Awesome! Will I be able to help you paint?"

"Sure, after school and maybe on Saturday."

"If your homework is done," Claire clarified. She turned to Ben. "Let's run by the grocery store and grab something for dinner."

"Sounds good," Ben agreed.

Claire pulled to the curb in front of Lita's Bakery. As usual, Lita Tanner was sitting on the bench in front of her store. She smiled when she saw the familiar minivan pull up.

"Mom, can I go to Lita's?" Mica asked.

"Sure," she answered. "Ben and I will grab a few things at the market, and you can meet us back here at the van."

Ben spoke up quickly. "I wanted to go to Lita's too."

"Fine, you two sweet hounds go ahead." Claire said and walked across the street to the grocery store.

"Well, if it isn't two of the handsomest men in Dunquin Cove," Lita said as Ben and Mica approached her. "What can I do for you gentlemen today?"

"Cookies," Mica said.

"And something for dessert," Ben added.

"Well, get yourselves right on in there," Lita said. "Howard was in that kitchen all morning just baking away."

Mica flung the door open and, entranced by the aroma of fresh-baked goods, practically floated inside. Ben held the door open for Lita and entered behind her.

"Always smells so good in here," he commented.

Lita smiled. "Like Howard always says, you gain five pounds just from smellin'."

Mica ran to the glass case. "Got any oatmeal-chocolate chip cookies, Mr. Tanner?"

Howard Tanner wiped his hands on the front of his apron as he walked around behind the counter. "You bet I do, young fella." He slid the glass door open. "How many can I get you?"

Mica looked over his shoulder at Ben.

"A dozen, I guess," Ben said.

Mica returned his attention to the long metal tray of cookies. "A dozen, please, Mr. Tanner."

Howard grabbed a white box made from thin cardboard off of the counter behind him. "Coming right up."

"How about that apple pie there too, Howard?" Ben asked.

"You got it."

As Ben pulled his money clip from his pocket, Lita spoke up. "Mica, Howard will knock 10 percent off your purchase if ya take that garbage out and throw it in the dumpster for me."

"Sure," Mica responded, eager to help out. He ran to the back door, picked up the garbage bag, and threw it over his shoulder.

"Make sure you lock the door when you come back in, Mica," Howard called out.

"Okay, Mr. Tanner."

Howard loaded the pie into another box and tied both boxes shut with string. "Here ya go, Ben," he said, sliding the boxes across the counter. "That'll be fourteen bucks."

Mica walked back into the room.

"Did ya lock the door, young fella?" Howard asked.

"Yes, sir."

"Lita, honey, will you just run back there and make sure it's locked?"

Lita started toward the door. "You're just being paranoid, Howard."

"Paranoid?" Ben asked. "Why?"

"Oh, he saw someone out in the alley the other night, and now he's locking doors and wants security lights put out in the alley."

"Hey, you can never be too careful," Howard said. "He was probably casing the bakery."

"Casing the bakery," Lita repeated with a little chuckle of annoyance. "I think someone's been watching way too many cop shows on the old boob tube."

"Who was out there?" Mica asked.

"Yeah," said Ben, "and what were they doing?"

Howard shrugged. "I don't know. He was just standing there. Couldn't tell who it was. There's no lighting out there, and he was wearing dark clothes and a dark ski cap."

"He say anything?" Ben asked.

"Nope. Just looked over at me when he heard the back door open, then he turned and walked around the corner onto Shore Drive. Kind of creeped me out so I didn't follow him__, just threw the garbage in the dumpster and came back in."

"Huh," Ben said.

"Now he's got some company coming and putting in lights and cameras," Lita said as she pushed open the double swinging doors and walked into the kitchen. The doors swung shut behind her. "Was a time when we didn't worry about locking the door__, used to go home at night with money still in the register," she called out. "Now my husband is a nervous Nellie just because of one little incident."

Howard looked wounded. "I resent that! Sure, Dunquin Cove is a quiet little burg, but it's not immune to crime. It's an ever-changing world out there, and I just want to feel safe, that's all."

"Then get a dog," Lita suggested. "Better yet, a gun. Heckuva lot cheaper than all this security nonsense.

Ben ignored the bickering couple. "Let me guess," he said to Howard. "Petrelli and Pert."

"Yeah, that's the guys," said Howard. "You get a door hanger too?"

Ben nodded. "How much are they charging you?"

"I don't know yet. They're coming tomorrow afternoon to give me an estimate."

"Howard, can you do me a favor?"

"Sure. What is it?"

"Before you sign anything, can you let me have a quick look at the contract?"

"Sure, Ben. Do you think these guys aren't on the up and up?"

"I'm not saying that, but you can never be too careful." Ben turned to Mica. "Let's head on over to the store and see what's taking your mother so long."

Lita pushed open the kitchen door as Ben and Mica were leaving. "Thanks, boys. Have a nice night and tell Claire we said hi."

Ben gave a wave over his shoulder. "Will do, Lita, thanks."

Chapter Nine

Claire pulled the minivan into the driveway. Marvin was gone, as was Cobb and his lawn chair. The ladder had been taken down and was now resting horizontally against the B&B's foundation on the side of the house. The scrapers, chisel, and wire brush were lying in a neat pile on the front steps. When Ben climbed from the van, he pulled the piece of paper from his pocket and read the phone number. "I think I'll give this woman a call," he said as he walked across the yard. Remembering the groceries, he pivoted. "As soon as I carry in the bags."

Claire popped the back hatch and Ben and Mica each grabbed a couple bags and took them inside, setting them on the dining room table.

"You want help putting these away?" Ben asked.

"No, that's okay. You go make your call."

Ben walked to the hallway, picked up the phone and dialed. "Hello?" came a woman's voice after the fourth ring.

"Hi. Is this Peg O'Leary?"

"Yes, it is."

"This is Ben Dunning. Maude Everly over at the hardware store gave me your number. She said you were looking for a painter."

"I am."

"Good! I was wondering if I could come over and have a look at the job and give you a price."

"Dunning?" Peg asked. "I know a Claire Dunning. Are you one of her kin?"

"Yes, I'm her brother-in-law."

"And you're a painter?"

Ben paused for a moment. "Yes. As a matter of fact I'm painting a big old Victorian right now."

"I guess you can come over and have a look if you would like. When can you be here?"

"How's six o'clock sound?"

"Sounds good to me."

"Can I get your address?" Ben asked.

Peg laughed. "I guess that would help you find the place. It's 411 Lake Street."

"Okay, thank you very much. I'll see you at six."

Ben hung up the phone and walked into the kitchen.

"Everything go okay?" Claire asked. She was on her tip toes putting a can of tomato soup in the cupboard.

"I gotta be over there at six," Ben answered. He walked up behind Claire and put his arm around her waist and with his other hand he pulled back her hair and kissed her on the neck. She turned and kissed him.

"That's gross," Mica commented. He walked into the room and started jostling grocery bags around. "Where are the cookies?"

Ben pulled Claire in closer to him. "I think they're still in the van. Why don't you run out and grab them while I kiss your mom a few more times?"

Mica turned and walked out of the kitchen. "Ugh, I'm going to have nightmares."

Claire laughed and pulled Ben in for one more peck on the lips. "Let me get these groceries put away, and then I'll start dinner. Did you want to eat before you look at the job or after?"

"Either is fine but, I have a feeling Mica and I will be loading up on cookies when he gets back in here."

Claire pulled a box of spaghetti from a bag and sat it on the counter next to the stove. "Maybe we should just have the cookies for dinner."

"And rob you of the opportunity to make us a wonderful dinner? I wouldn't do that to you."

Claire placed a jar of Ragu next to the spaghetti. "Thanks, you're always thinking about my needs," she said sarcastically. "I better get started on the sauce."

"Let me guess. An old recipe of your aunt's?"

"That's right," Claire replied. "One cup of twist off the lid and a tablespoon of pour it into the pan."

Ben smiled. "That never gets old." He turned and went out of the kitchen. "What's taking that boy so long? I need a cookie."

"He's probably sitting on the porch eating them," Claire called out.

Ben started down the hall. "He better not be."

When Ben got to the front door he pulled back the curtain to see Mica, holding the box of cookies, standing beside the road and talking to someone in a late model, black Lincoln. He opened the door and walked out onto the porch. As Ben watched, the man in the driver's seat leaned forward and looked past Mica as he talked, then he leaned back again. Even from that distance Ben could see the sharpness and focus in the man's eyes, like a falcon searching a field, from high above, for its prey.

Ben walked down the steps and out to the road. He put his hand on Mica's shoulder.

"You must be Mr. Dunning," the driver said.

He had a shaved head and a bulldog-ish face highlighted by a unibrow, no neck, and a linebacker's body squeezed into a dark gray suit. Ben noticed that his jacket sleeves were stretched tight around his massive arms. He had a permanent smile and even seemed to continue smiling as he spoke.

"I am," Ben replied, playing along.

"I'm Marco Gannon," the driver said, and then nodded toward the passenger seat. "This here is Mr. Petrelli." Gannon said the name Petrelli as though Ben should be impressed.

Ben bent down and looked at Petrelli, who stared straight ahead and said nothing.

Petrelli was a big man too, but not as muscular. Years ago, when he took the orders, he was probably built more like Gannon, but now, after a few years of *giving* the orders, he had become softer and pudgier, like a high school jock at his twenty year reunion. He, too, wore a suit__, black, and more expensive. His jacket had been removed sometime during the day and was folded over the back of the seat.

"The boy says you're a painter," Gannon remarked.

Mica blurted out, "He asked what you and Mom did for—"

"Why don't you run on inside, I'll be right in," Ben interrupted.

Mica turned and ran up the walkway.

"You a house painter or some kind of an artist or something?" Gannon asked.

Ben looked up from the car and glanced around the street; he had a bad feeling. "Listen, fellas, whatever it is you're selling, I'm not buying, so why don't you gentlemen have a nice day and move on."

The permanent smile finally left Gannon's face. "What we're selling, Dunning, is security and peace of mind."

Ben put his hand on top of the car. "Like I said, I'm not buying."

"People always think that … until it's too late. It sure would be a shame if something happened to that little boy, or to his beautiful blonde mother."

Ben felt the rage build inside him but it didn't show on the outside. "Don't you worry, I'll keep my family safe. You just worry about your own safety."

Gannon's smile returned and his bulldog mouth opened, but before he could speak Petrelli tapped on the dashboard. Gannon looked over and his passenger pointed straight ahead.

"You have a nice day, Ben," Gannon said. He put the car in drive and sped off down the road. Ben watched as they drove to Main Street and took a right.

When Ben turned around he could see Claire and Mica with the curtain pulled back, watching him. He smiled and waved.

"Who was that?" Claire asked when she opened the door.

"Just a couple of guys asking directions," Ben said.

"Did you tell them what they needed to know?"

"I told them," Ben answered. "Let's just hope they were listening."

Chapter Ten

Ben scooped up his last bite of apple pie, shoved it in his mouth, and then laid his fork on the empty plate. He leaned back in his chair and rubbed his belly. "I think I may have over done it," he announced.

Mica copied Ben's motions and said, "Yeah, me too."

Claire slid her plate toward Mica. "You'd better not be too full to help me clear the table and do the dishes."

"I would, Mom, but me and Ben have to go look at a painting job."

"Oh you do, do you?"

"Yeah, and besides, that's woman's work," Mica informed his mother.

Claire's eyes shot to Ben.

Oh crap! Ben thought and threw up his hands in surrender.

Claire returned her glare to her son. "And where exactly did you hear that?"

Mica knew he was in trouble and chose his words carefully. "Um … everywhere. I … uh … mean that, you know, dishes, laundry, cleaning the house, stuff like that. That's woman's work."

Claire lowered her brow. "And what would you two caveman consider man's work?"

"You two? Don't get me involved!" Ben protested. "Mica, answer your mother's question."

"I guess fixing things, working on the house, things like that," Mica answered, his voice now a little shaky and much less confident.

"Well, let me tell you something, mister! In this house, we don't have *man* jobs and *woman* jobs, but what we do have is grown-up jobs and kid jobs. And because of your little attitude, for the next week the kid job is going to be clearing the table and doing the dishes every night."

"So, does that mean you'll be helping to scrape and paint the house, since it's not a *man's* job?" Mica asked angrily.

Ben tried to hide his smile.

"Two weeks," Claire said.

"Awe, man." Mica stood and looked to Ben for support.

"Hey, pal, you made your bed, you gotta lie in it," Ben said.

Mica began clearing the table. "Thanks."

*****

Ben glanced up at the clock over the fireplace; it was five-fifteen. Claire sat in the red chair next to the fireplace, its plush hugeness practically swallowing her. As usual, she was engrossed by a mystery novel. She could feel Ben's eyes upon her and looked up from her book.

"What?"

"Nothing."

Claire smiled. "Why are you staring at me?"

"Because you're beautiful." He stood, walked over to her, and kissed her. "I love you."

"I love you too. Is everything okay?" She took the bookmark from the arm of the chair, placed it in the book, and closed it.

"Everything is fine. Do you think Mica's done with those dishes? I was going to take him with me to look at that job."

"I'm sure he's done. I don't know what he's up to now."

Ben walked from the parlor into the hall, where he could see Mica sitting at the dining room table doing his homework.

"Hey," he said, snatching the van keys off of the phone stand. "Did you want to go over and look at the painting job with me?"

Mica jumped up from the table. "Yes!"

"Well, let's go." Ben turned, walked to the screen door, and pushed it open. Mica was right behind him when he went down the stairs.

Mica ran to the van and jumped in. When Ben opened the door Mica said, "This is awesome! I've never looked at a potential job before. Have you?"

The only thing Ben knew about his previous life was what he had done for a living, so he knew he must have looked at a job before. He also knew that looking at a painting job was probably a lot different than looking at a job to end someone's life.

In the past few months, Ben had tried not to think about his old life for fear of remembering something that he didn't want to remember. Recently, however, as he grew closer to Claire and Mica, he caught himself day dreaming, it was starting to get the best of him. He wondered how long he had been a hitman, what caused him to turn to a life of violence … and, most importantly how many men, or even women, for that matter, he had killed.

"Ben?" Mica said softly. "Ben, is everything okay?"

Ben suddenly snapped out of his thoughts; before he knew it, he had driven three blocks. He looked over at Mica, who was staring at him. "Yeah," he answered. "Everything is fine."

"Did you hear what I said?"

"No, sorry. What did you say?"

"I asked you if you had ever looked at a job before."

Ben looked back at the road. "No, I don't think so." He took a left onto Flagg Street.

"You have to think up a name," Mica said.

"A name?"

"Yeah, you know, like Dunquin Cove Painting or something like that."

Ben laughed. "Why don't you work on that?" He made a left on Lake Street and started watching the house numbers. When he came to 411 he pulled to the curb.

Peg O'Leary was standing in her front yard with her back to the road, studying her home. When she heard the van pull up, she turned around. Ben and Mica climbed from the van and made their way across the street.

"You're right on time, Mr. Dunning," Peg said.

"Pleased to meet you, Ms. O'Leary," Ben responded, extending his hand.

Peg took his hand and gave it a gentle shake. "Make it Peg. This must be Claire's boy."

Mica smiled and stuck out his hand.

Ben said, "This is Mica."

Mica smiled and said, "It's nice to meet you, ma'am."

"You can call me Peg, too, little fella."

Mica nodded. "Okay, ma'am—, I mean, Peg."

Ben looked up at the old Victorian home. "Wow, big house," he commented. He started walking around the home as he took it all in. The wooden clapboards and trim around the windows was in great need of scraping and painting. The old house probably had wooden shutters in its early days but they had since been removed and replaced with vinyl ones—easier to maintain probably, but lacking character. The dentil work and the large columns that supported the porch roof were in great shape and probably didn't need as much scraping. Ben noticed that the entire main roof, except for the turret, still had the original slate tiles.

Peg followed along. "Yeah, too big," she informed him. "Raised four girls and two boys in this house.

They've all grown up and moved away. And my husband, he passed away three years ago. Now it's just me and the cat, and we don't even use half the rooms. Can't bring myself to sell her, though. I was born in this house and I'll probably die in this house."

When they got to the backyard, Ben gazed around the property. "The garage too?" he asked.

"Yup. The garage, and that old shed over there," she answered, pointing to the lopsided building squatting in an overgrown corner of the yard.

Crap, Ben thought, *I should have brought a notebook and pen, maybe even a tape measure.* He hoped she wouldn't notice his unprofessionalism. So far he had gotten off easy; she hadn't even asked to see photos of his work, or for references. Ben was glad that Dunquin Cove typified small town values, like trusting your neighbors.

"Okay," he said. "Maude Everly over at the hardware store said you looked at color samples this morning. Did you pick anything out?"

"Not yet. Do you need to know the colors now?"

"No, just how many different colors."

"Same as now," she answered. "The house itself one color, the trim another, and the doors and shutters a third color. The garage and shed the same color as the house."

"Okay, sounds good. I'll write you up an estimate and get back to you in a couple of days."

"Can you give me a ballpark figure now?" Peg asked.

Ben thought for a moment; he had no idea how much it should cost to paint a house. He looked over at Mica, who shrugged, and then back to Peg. "I'll tell you what, Peg, if you want to pay in cash and give me half down, I'll do it for ten thousand."

"Wow, that's all?"

Crap, I should have went higher. "Yeah. Is that okay?"

"That sounds great! Let me run in the house and grab you some money. When can you start?"

"I have to finish the job I'm on, so probably in three weeks."

"Sounds good," she said and went inside.

Mica looked up at Ben. "You should have went higher."

Chapter Eleven

Claire watched Mica as he ran down the sidewalk, through the gate, and jumped on the waiting school bus. The driver gave Claire a quick wave and pulled the lever that shut the door. She pushed the front door shut and walked into the dining room.

Ben sat at the dining room table reading that morning's copy of the *Dunquin Crier* and sipping a cup of coffee. The faint sound of Gordon Lightfoot singing "Carefree Highway" could be heard from the radio in the kitchen.

"Sox are in first place__, of course, we're only three weeks in," he said as Claire entered the room.

"Did they win last night?" Claire asked.

"No, they lost, four to three."

"What time did you come to bed?"

"I think the game ended a little after ten."

"We should go to a game this summer," Claire suggested.

Ben folded the paper and laid it on the table. "Yeah, maybe."

He wondered if it would really be safe for him to take Claire and Mica into Boston. What if the wrong person recognized him. A simple little trip into Boston could endanger them. He knew eventually he would have to face his past. He couldn't live forever with the fear of something happening to Claire and Mica because of him, because of something he may have done. Claire's voice suddenly pulled him back.

"I'm going to run over to Farmwell's and grab Mica a pair of pants, and then I have to run a few more errands. Do you want to come with me?"

Ben took a drink of his coffee. "No, you go ahead. I'm going to try and get some more scraping done today."

"Okay." Claire grabbed her sweater off of the coatrack and slipped it on. "Shouldn't be too long."

Ben stood and they kissed. "Love you," he said.

"I love you too." Claire had just opened the front door when she turned around and asked, "Hey, do you want to meet me at The Cove a little after noon for lunch?"

"Sure," Ben answered. "I wanted to run by and see if Artie had gotten the new tire in. I'll stop by there after lunch."

"Okay, I'll see you then," she said and walked out the door.

When the door shut Ben stood motionless, waiting to hear the van pull away. When he was satisfied that Claire was gone, he turned and went through the kitchen to the cellar stairs.

At the bottom of the stairs he reached his hand up over his head, and behind a floor joist. On top of the foundation wall, he grabbed a small envelope he had stashed there months earlier, and opened it. He sat down on the second step of the stairs and pulled out the envelope's contents: three credit cards and a driver's license. Two of the credit cards had the name Charles E. Hewitt; the name on the other card was Jason Stone. Ben stuck the credit cards back in the envelope and stared at the driver's license. The photo was of Ben but the name was Wesley J. Hargreaves, and the address was 37 Garden Street, Medford, Massachusetts.

Ben stuffed the driver's license back in with the credit cards. He thought back to the day, last fall, when he and Cam Owens had driven three miles out of town to the field where he awoke after the car accident and his new life began. He remembered finding the money clip in the tall grass with the $570 inside, along with the cards and license. Ben smiled to himself as he recalled holding on to the money as long as he could to buy Christmas presents for Claire and Mica.

He closed the envelope and returned it to its hiding place.

Chapter Twelve

Claire had driven around the block and parked her van in front of Farmwell's Department Store, across the street from Lenny's Garage. Main Street was bustling—by Dunquin Cove's humble standards—with the steady coming and going of locals and the odd tourist.

She stood at the front of the van searching through her purse for quarters to feed the parking meter. The sound of a car driving by caught her attention, and she looked over at the black Lincoln pulling into Lenny's. She recognized it immediately as the car that had stopped in front of her B&B the day before.

"I got it, Claire," came a voice from the sidewalk.

She glanced over to see Officer Chet Rose pulling change from his pocket and placing it into the old fashioned meter. The red expired flag flipped out of view with a buzz, and the needle shot up to the one-hour mark.

Chet was a local boy, and not only had he spent the last few years on the Dunquin Cove police force, but before that, he had been a student of Claire's husband Clay's when he taught at the college. During breaks from school, Chet would do odd jobs around the B&B for extra money.

"Thanks, Chet," Claire said as she zipped her purse closed. "But I won't need that long."

"Oh, I'm just paying it forward for the next customer."

Claire grinned mischievously. "Sure you don't want to chalk my tire, just in case? Must be some sort of ticket quota Dunquin Cove's finest have to meet."

Chet feigned indignation. "Now, Claire, you know we never stoop that low. So how's everything going? Didn't see much of you through the winter."

"I stay inside as much as possible in the winter, Chet. You know that." Claire returned her attention to the Lincoln across the street. She watched as two men got out of the car, the passenger went inside the office while the driver waited outside the door. "Chet, what do you know about those guys?"

Chet glanced over at Lenny's. "What guys?"

"The ones that just pulled up in the black car and went into the garage."

Chet shrugged. "I don't know much about them. I know they're in security … cameras, burglar alarms, things like that. They're opening an office and store down the street where the old gift shop was."

"They seem to be everywhere all of a sudden. They were at my house yesterday, and Ben said they are installing a security system at Lita's bakery. Now they're over at Lenny's."

Chet laughed. "There's no crime against working hard and being ambitious, Claire. Besides, it's always a good thing when new business comes to town."

"I guess," Claire agreed.

"Speaking of new businesses, I hear we have a new house painter in town."

"How did you hear about that?"

Chet turned and resumed his trek down the sidewalk. "Small town, Claire, very small town."

Claire swung her purse up over her shoulder and turned back for one last look across the street. The bulky man in the too-tight suit standing at the door raised his hand and waved. "Good morning, Mrs. Dunning. Beautiful day!" he shouted.

Claire hesitantly put up her hand in a half-wave, turned, and went into the store.

*****

A half hour later, when Claire exited Farmwell's, the black Lincoln was no longer at Lenny's Garage. Artie was pumping gas into a silver Chevy sedan; he looked up, saw Claire, and waved. Claire smiled and waved back. Artie held up his finger, telling Claire to hold on for a second. She opened the van door and placed her purse and the shopping bags on the back seat, closed the door, and waited.

When Artie was finished with his customer, he ran into the garage and came back out rolling a brand new tire on a rim.

"Tire's all fixed, Claire," he hollered as he made his way across the street. "Pop the back hatch, and I'll toss it in there for you."

"Thanks, Artie," said Claire after the tire was loaded. "What do I owe you?"

"Don't you worry about it, I'll hit Ben up later. Besides, Lenny mentioned something about getting the garage painted. Maybe he can work something out with Ben."

Claire shook her head. "Wow, word spreads fast. He's not painting anything until the B&B is done."

Artie laughed. "Just tell him to stop by when he gets a chance."

"I will, Artie. We're having lunch today at The Cove. Join us?"

"I'm not gonna spoil you two lovebirds' romantic idyll."

"Artie, you're a poet at heart.

Chapter Thirteen

Ben stood on the porch roof, scraping around one of the bedroom windows. After he scraped a section, he scrubbed it with the wire brush. *This isn't so hard to do*, he thought. *I could be a painter.*

"How's it going over there, neighbor?" came Marvin's voice from his front porch. "Great day for painting a house."

"Sure is," Ben agreed. The weather was exactly the same as it was the day before, when the contrary old coot had deemed it too cold to paint.

Marvin walked down his front steps. "Let me grab my step ladder and scraper and I'll give you a hand."

"You don't have to do that, Marvin."

"I know I don't have to, I want to. What are neighbors for?"

That's what I've been wondering. Ben returned to his scraping, all the while wondering exactly how it was that he and Marvin went from being neighbors who barely spoke or saw each other to being best friends in just two days.

Marvin returned shortly with all the necessary tools for bothering a neighbor. He leaned the ladder against the house, climbed up on the third step, and began scraping.

Ben looked down from the roof. "I've already done that section, Marv."

Marvin stopped scraping for a second and gave the wall a sideways look. "Really? It doesn't look like it. Let me just get some of these spots you missed."

Ben shook his head. "Yeah. You do that."

"Any places you miss will just peel off later," Marv commented. "You gotta make sure every loose piece has been scraped away."

"I wish someone would scrape you away," Ben mumbled.

"What's that?"

"I said, 'sure is a great day.'"

*****

"What time is it, Marv?" Ben asked.

"Why, ya got a date?" Marv hollered back.

"As a matter of fact I do."

Marv looked at his watch, a drug store Timex with giant numbers that could be read from outer space. "It's eleven-fifty."

"I'm supposed to meet Claire at The Cove for lunch. I better head over there."

"Good idea, I think I'll go on in and make myself a sandwich." Marv looked at his watch again. "Meet back out here in an hour or so?"

Ben started down the ladder. "I should be back around then." When he got to the bottom of the ladder, he turned and added, "Hey, Marv, thanks for all your help here."

"Don't thank me, we'll probably be doing mine next," Marv grumbled.

Ben looked over at Marv's house. It was long overdue for a coat of paint. "Sounds good to me."

Chapter Fourteen

"Yo, Benjamin!" a familiar voice bellowed as Ben walked through the front doors of The Cove. It was Curt Holliday, a regular holding court from his favorite stool at the bar, the one with a perfect imprint of his skinny ass.

Ben scanned the dining room for Claire and then the bar; she was nowhere in sight. He went to the bar, pulled out a stool, and sat down. "What's up, Curt?"

"Same old thing, Ben. Here for lunch?"

Ben looked at the clock up over the bar. "Yeah, I'm supposed to be meeting Claire.

Curt held up his hand. "Marcia, grab Ben a beer, would ya?"

"Comin' right up," In ten seconds flat, she had grabbed a glass from under the bar, filled it under the Guinness tap, and sat it in front of Ben on a cardboard coaster.

"Fastest bartender in Maine," said Curt admiringly.

"And always a perfect head," Marcia added. She caught both men's devilish grins. "I'm talking about the beer, you smartasses."

"Of course you were, Marcia," Ben said, reaching into his pocket.

"I've got this one," Curt offered, sliding a few ones forward on the bar.

"Thanks, Curt."

Marcia took the money and stuck it in the open till. "How did you feel Tuesday morning, Ben? You left here in pretty rough shape."

Curt laughed out loud. "I'll say he did. I offered you a ride home, buddy, but you said you wanted to walk."

Ben took a sip of his beer. "I sure as hell wasn't going to get a ride from you; you were just as bad as me." He returned his attention to Marcia and pointed a finger at her. "And you, don't ever let him bring that shit in here again."

"Oh, well," Curt said. "Suddenly someone doesn't like moonshine."

"No, I don't."

"Ya sure seemed to love it *that* night."

"I just didn't know any better," Ben explained, as he watched the door in the mirror behind the bar. He took another drink of his beer, then excused himself, and made his way down the hall that led to the men's room.

When he got to the end of the hall he looked at the bulletin board outside the restroom door. The flyer he had seen months earlier was still there. The boldface headline HAVE YOU SEEN THIS MAN appeared above a grainy photo that, if one squinted, looked vaguely human. Ben remembered the first time he saw the flyer. He remembered wondering if anyone had found the man, and now six months later, he wondered the same thing. He also couldn't help but wonder if somewhere there was a poster with his photo on it.

"So, I hear you're going into business for yourself," Marcia said, when Ben had returned and climbed back on his barstool.

"How did you know that?"

"Honey, I'm the bartender__, the bartender knows everything."

"I told her," Curt let on.

"That too," Marcia said.

The door opened, and Ben's eyes went back to the mirror. It wasn't Claire. He checked the clock again. *Where is she?*

The phone rang and Marcia picked it up. "The Cove Restaurant and Bar. How may I help you?" She listened for a moment. "Oh my God. When did it happen?"

The door opened again. Ben looked at the mirror. It was Claire.

"Okay," Marcia said. "If Mac comes in, I'll have him call you." She hung up the phone.

Ben stood up from the stool, picked up his glass, and waved to Claire.

"Something wrong, Marcia?" Curt asked.

"That was Chet. They found Mac Reynold's dog over on Flagg Street. Said it looks like he was hit by a car."

"Dead?" Curt asked.

"He didn't say, but I assume so."

Ben met Claire halfway across the dining room. "Did you want to sit at the bar?" she asked.

"No," Ben answered. "Let's get a table. There's something I need to talk to you about."

"Oh, Mr. Mysterious!" Claire said. She caught Ben's serious expression and the smile ran away from her face. She ordered a glass of white wine for herself, and they each ordered a burger. When the waitress left the table, Ben took a deep breath and exhaled slowly.

"Claire," he began, "everything here is going great. I love you, and I love Mica." He looked around. "I even love this crazy town." He paused.

Claire tasted her wine. "But?"

"But I have to leave for a while."

She sat her drink down slowly and stared into the glass. "For how long?"

"I don't know. There's something I haven't told you. Back in the fall, when I first came here, I woke up in a field outside of town."

"I know that."

"But what I didn't tell you is that I had Cam Owens take me back out to the field a couple days later to have a look around. While we were out there I found a money clip. Inside the money clip were a few credit cards and a driver's license. I hid them in the cellar."

Claire nodded her head. "I know, I found them a few months ago."

"Why didn't you say anything?"

"Because I figured when you were ready, you would talk about it. I guess I was right."

"I guess you were," Ben agreed.

"So what now?"

"The driver's license has my picture on it with another name and address. I think that address is the best place to start."

"To start what?"

"Claire, I have to find out everything: who I was, what I've done, where I came from. I may have a family somewhere out there that's looking for me. Those two goons that came after Bob Phillips back in the fall told me I didn't have any children, and that I wasn't married. But what about a father or a mother?"

Claire was silent. She turned her head toward the front of the restaurant and stared out the window.

Ben reached across the table and took her hand in his. "Claire, I'll be back. I have to do this. If I don't, my life— our life—here will never be complete if part of me is somewhere else."

"How long?"

"A few days, tops."

Claire slowly nodded her head. "I don't want to lose you, I love you."

Ben squeezed her hand. "And I love you. That's why I'll be back."

Chapter Fifteen

After lunch, Ben walked Claire back to the van. "Did you want a ride back to the house?" she asked.

"No," he answered. "I'm going to walk up the street and see Artie for a minute and then I'll walk home."

"Oh, yeah, I saw Artie this morning. He put the new tire in the back and told me to tell you to stop over when you got a chance."

They kissed and Claire climbed into the van. Ben watched as she pulled away from the curb and turned the corner onto Dunquin Lane. He turned and made his way up the street.

*****

Ben rapped his knuckles on the doorjamb. "Artie, you in there?" he called out. There was no answer. "Artie!" He walked through the office and into the garage.

Artie had a Buick LaSabre up on the lift, and his head was stuck up under the engine. Ben didn't see him.

"Artie!"

Artie jumped, smashing his head against the under carriage. "Jesus Christ!" he shouted.

"Oh, sorry, didn't see you there."

"Don't sneak up on a guy like that—you scared the shit out of me." Artie yanked a rag from his back pocket, wiped it across his forehead, and then inspected the rag for blood; there was none. He wiped his hands and returned the rag to his pocket. "You here to settle up?"

"I am."

"Come on in the office." Artie sat down behind the desk and began shuffling paperwork around. "Lenny mentioned something about having the garage painted. Would you be interested in a job?"

"Sure, probably wouldn't be able to get to it until the first part of June, though."

Lenny should be around tomorrow afternoon," Artie replied. "Why don't you stop by then and he can talk to you about it." He pushed a few more papers here and there and then slumped back in his chair in defeat. "Hell's bells, I can't find your bill anyway. Remember what I quoted you?"

"One seventy-nine, I believe."

"Sounds right."

Ben reached into his pocket, pulled out a thick wad of greenbacks, and peeled off a few bills. "By the way, I wanted to talk to you about the Ford you got for sale out there."

Artie's eyes lit up at the sight of Ben's roll. "She's a *beaut*, aint she? Ya interested?"

"Sure thing. You said thirty-five hundred?" Ben counted out a series of fifties, twenties, tens, and a five and tossed them on the desk. "There. Cash on the ole barrelhead. But you'll have to do me a favor."

Artie picked up the cash. "What's that, Ben?"

"I need you to let me keep those plates on her for a few days till I can get to the DMV."

"I'll tell you what, you take the truck now, and when you're on your way over to the tag office, swing by here and I'll sign over the title."

Ben reached out and he and Artie shook hands. "Thanks, Artie."

"Thank *you*."

*****

Marvin was already back at work by the time Ben pulled his new truck into the driveway. When Ben climbed out of the truck, Marvin turned and tapped on his watch.

"I know, I know," Ben apologized. "I had a few things to do at Lenny's."

Marvin climbed down from his step ladder and walked over to the vehicle. "I'm guessing that borrowing Artie's truck was one of those things."

"Nope. *Buying* Artie's truck was one of those things." Ben slapped his hand on the hood of the truck. "What do you think?"

"I think you should have bought a Chevy."

"Of course you do."

Marv returned to his ladder and continued scraping. "I'm just saying that if it was me I would have bought a Chevy." You know what F-O-R-D stands for, don't ya?"

"No, but I bet you'll tell me."

"Found On Road Dead," Marvin cackled.

Ben ignored him and went into the house.

"When I got home, your partner was already hard at work," Claire said when Ben entered the house. "He's quite a worker."

"He's quite a something," Ben said. "Would you like to come out and see my new truck?"

Claire cocked her head. "Your new *what*?"

"I bought Artie's truck with O'Leary's deposit money."

Claire got up from the couch. "Okay, let's have a look." She followed Ben back to the front door. "You're really serious about this painting business aren't you?"

"I gotta do something."

"Well, your next purchase should be a cell phone. Howard down at the bakery called and wants you to come over and look at an estimate or something."

"I'll stop over before they close." Ben led the way to the truck. "What do you think?" he asked, smiling like a lobotomy patient and waving his arms in his best Vanna White impression.

"It's a truck," Claire answered.

"He should have bought a Chevy," Marv hollered from his ladder.

Chapter Sixteen

Howard Tanner was hunched over behind the glass counter, placing cookies into a box with tongs, when Ben walked through the door of the bakery. The lighted sign out front had been turned off but the plastic sign on the door was still turned to OPEN.

"Closing up for the night, Howard?" Ben inquired.

Howard glanced up at the clock. "Another glorious work day coming to an end," he stated blandly. "Flip that sign around to CLOSED, will ya?"

Ben did so and said, "Those guys stop by and give you an estimate?"

"Sure did. Seem like real nice guys, very knowledgeable."

"I would hope so."

"Hold on, let me finish this and I'll grab the estimate for you."

"Eating one of those peanut butter cookies might help me hold on while you finish."

Howard glanced up through the glass at Ben, grabbed a cookie with the tongs, slapped a wedge of wax paper under it, and tossed it up on top of the counter. "Have at it."

Ben took the treat, walked to the front of the shop, and gazed out the window as he ate. "Quiet night," he observed.

"For a few more weeks," Howard said. "Then the tourists start flocking in."

The lights in the grocery store went out, and few seconds later John Morgan, the butcher, came out the front door, he was smoking a big cigar. He turned, pulled a ring of keys off of his belt loop, and locked up. When he turned back around, he took a big drag on the stogie and blew smoke rings into the air while rocking on his heels. He looked down the street toward the ocean and ambled up the street, the very picture of a man content with his lot in life.

"Okay, all done," Howard said.

Ben turned and Howard handed him a piece of paper. "Just one page, huh?" He sat down in one of the chairs along the wall, laid the sheet on the table, and began reading. When he was done he flipped it over and looked at the back, which was blank, and then placed it back on the table.

"What do you think?" Howard asked. "Is it a good price?"

"I don't know, Howard. The initial price for installing the cameras, lights, monitor, and the rest of it seems fine. But what about this monthly payment they're talking about?"

"Gannon said that was a maintenance fee."

"I know, but it says here you start paying that the first month."

"He said that's just in case something breaks or has to be replaced. Any work that has to be done is free."

"It's not free, Howard, because you'll be paying this maintenance fee even if nothing breaks."

"I get what you're saying. It just seemed like a good deal when he was here talking about it."

"He's a salesman, Howard—they make everything seem like a good deal. In my opinion, I would pass. There's nothing on this list that you and I couldn't do for half the price, and without a monthly maintenance fee."

Howard picked up the paper and stared at it for a second. "Yeah, I guess you're right, Ben, maybe I will pass on this."

Ben stood up. "However, I will need a maintenance fee of one more of those cookies."

"It's a deal, but only if you help me load these boxes into the van."

"I can do that," Ben said as he walked over and picked up four of the boxes. "Where are these going, anyway?"

Howard picked up the remaining boxes and followed Ben out of the store. "We donate a few baked goods to the food pantry down in York every week."

"That's a nice thing to do."

"Lita's idea."

Ben smiled. "Yeah, I figured."

Chapter Seventeen

Ben tossed a small backpack on the front seat of his truck. "A couple days, I promise," he said. He turned and put his arms around Claire. She laid her head on his chest, and he kissed the top of her head.

"I told Mica to come down and tell you goodbye," Claire said.

"I went into his room and talked to him this morning."

"What did you say?"

"I told him I had to run into Boston and get some things I had left there."

"When I went into his room last night he was working on a name for your painting business."

Ben smiled. "I told him to come up with something."

Claire lifted her head off Ben's chest and gave him a proper goodbye kiss.

"Whoa, I should go away more often."

"Don't joke," said Claire, looking into his eyes. "We can't lose you, Ben; we can't go through something like that again."

"I know."

They kissed one more time, and Ben climbed into his truck and drove down the street. Claire stood at the curb and watched until he was out of sight, turned, and walked slowly up the sidewalk. She went in and closed the door behind her.

"Mica!" she hollered up from the bottom of the stairs. "The school bus is going to be here any minute."

Mica's bedroom door shut seconds later. He rounded the newel post and started down the stairs with a piece of notebook paper in his hand. "Did Ben leave?"

"He just drove away."

"Shoot! I wanted to show him the logo I drew for the painting business."

Claire held out her hand. "Can I have a look?"

"Um, I guess." He handed it to his mother.

The crude logo, executed in Magic Marker, displayed the words DUNNING AND SON in a gentle arc with a pair of paintbrushes underneath, the handles crossed like broadswords. The entire thing was in red, Mica's favorite color. Claire studied the paper for a moment, her bottom lip quivered a little, and then looked back at her son.

"Do you think he'll like it?" Mica asked.

"I think he will love it." She handed the paper back to Mica.

"I'll be right back down," he explained. "I want to put it back on my desk."

Claire heard the brakes of the school bus squeal as it came to a stop out front. She opened the door and pushed open the screen, propping it open with her foot. Mica ran past her wearing his backpack. Claire had hoped for a kiss goodbye but didn't get one.

"I love you!" she hollered after him.

The little boy cocked his head around. His face contorted in embarrassment for a moment, and then, smiling, he mouthed the same sentiment back at her.

Chapter Eighteen

"Dammit," Ben said quietly and smacked the steering wheel with the palms of his hands. He had watched the temperature gauge slowly rise for the past ten minutes. He had hoped it was just a sticky thermostat and it would open up at any minute. But it didn't look like that was going to happen.

Ben flipped on his blinker when he saw the sign, FAST EDDIE'S, NEXT EXIT. He crossed the Massachusetts state line immediately after exiting I-95 and followed the signs to the truck stop. He checked the gas gauge. *Might as well get gas too*, he thought, and pulled up to the pumps.

"How are you today, sir?" the young man behind the register asked in a rote monotone.

"Good," Ben replied, laying a fifty dollar bill on the counter. "I'm going to fill 'er up." He glanced around the store. "Also, a couple gallons of anti-freeze."

The clerk grabbed the money and placed it on top of the till and punched a couple keys on the cash register.

"You're all set, sir. Antifreeze is stacked out front. Have a nice day"

"You really mean that, son?" Ben asked.

"The boy's face went blank. "Well, I uh—"

"Just messing with ya."

Ben went out the door, grabbed the antifreeze, and made his way back to the gas pumps just as a yellow Dodge Charger pulled in behind him, rap music blasting. The Charger tapped his bumper. Ben rolled his eyes, but said nothing.

The driver of the Charger put it in reverse. He backed up a few feet, shut off the engine, and then shoved open the door and climbed out. "If you were pulled up where you should be, I wouldn't have run into you," he said, running his fingers through his greasy black hair.

Ben removed his gas cap and inserted the nozzle. "No harm," he said.

The greaser walked up to the front of his car and looked at the bumper. "No harm, what do you mean *no harm*? There's a scratch in my bumper."

"Carl, just forget about it," his female passenger hollered. "Just get the gas and let's go."

"The greaser pointed his finger at the young woman. "You shut your fucking mouth, Maggie, or I'll come around there and shut it for you."

Ben pushed the lever forward to lock the nozzle in the open position and let go.

"Who's gonna pay for this, asshole?" Carl said, pointing at the bumper.

Ben glanced down at the bumper. The scratch wasn't even noticeable, but the kid wouldn't let up. He had a chip on his shoulder and Ben knew he was just looking for trouble.

Maggie stuck her head out of the window. "Carl, come on, he's not worth it."

"She's right, Carl, I'm not worth it," Ben said puckishly.

Carl shot around to the side of the car and slapped Maggie on the side of the head with the back of his hand. "I told you to keep your goddamn mouth shut, bitch!"

Ben turned and walked toward Carl. "Don't hit her again." His teeth were clenched.

Carl reached in with his left arm and back handed her again, harder this time. Her head snapped back against the headrest. "Ya mean like that?"

Ben moved closer. Carl pulled a 9mm out from under his shirt and yanked back the slide. Ben froze. The barrel of the gun was two feet from his face.

Carl reached back through the window and grabbed Maggie by the hair. "If I want to slap the shit outta my woman, I'll slap the shit outta my woman." He let go of her hair and moved toward Ben, the barrel trained on his forehead. "And there's nothing you or anyone else can do about it."

Ben raised his arms slightly in a pretense of surrender. "Listen, pal, I don't want any trouble."

"Oh, really," Carl said, grinning. "A minute ago you were giving me orders, and now you don't want any trouble. Not such a big man now, are you?"

The gas nozzle suddenly snapped shut when the tank was full.

Carl's eyes shot to the nozzle. Ben grabbed the barrel of the gun with his left hand, turning it toward Carl. His right hand wrapped around Carl's as his thumb hit the magazine release button. Before the magazine hit the blacktop, Ben had twisted the gun from Carl's hand. His finger was on the trigger, the safety was off, and the barrel was pressed firmly against Carl's skull.

Carl didn't move. The grin on his face had been replaced by the fear in his eyes.

"There's one bullet left in this gun, Carl. I can eject it, or I can put it in your brain. It's your choice."

Carl's voice was shaky. "Do you know w-who I am?"

"I didn't know who you were when you pulled in here, but right now you're a shaking bag of shit." Ben grabbed the back of Carl's head and pushed the gun even harder against his forehead.

"My father i—" was all Carl got out before Ben brought the grip of the pistol down on the top of his head. Carl's legs buckled and he hit the ground.

Ben ejected the last shell and tossed the gun into the tall grass at the edge of the parking lot. "Do you need a ride somewhere?" he asked Maggie.

She quickly opened the car door and jumped out. With the red heels she was wearing, she was the same height as Ben. She wore faded jeans and a tight white T-shirt with the Superman logo stretched over breasts that had probably been purchased by Carl. *Carl's going to want them back at some point*, Ben thought.

Maggie ran her long red fingernails through her shoulder-length blonde hair. "My mother lives in Dorchester," she said.

"Get in," Ben said. He glanced over at the building; the cashier was standing in the window, the phone in his hand. Ben went back inside.

"Do you have a map of the Boston area?"

The clerk pointed a shaking finger at a rack behind Ben.

Ben turned, grabbed one, and placed in on the counter. "How much?"

"No charge."

"Well, thank you."

"No problem."

"Oh, and did you call the cops?"

"I was going to," the clerk said. His lip quivered as he spoke.

"What are you going to tell them?" Ben asked, reaching for his money clip.

"Um … uh, I, um saw this thug pull up in a yellow Charger and pull a gun on some guy in a truck, and the guy in the truck took it away from him and hit him with it?"

"Good so far. What type of truck was the guy driving?"

"A Ford?"

Ben slowly shook his head "no" as he counted out two hundred dollars.

"A Chevy Tahoe?"

Ben nodded "yes" and laid the money on the counter. "What did the guy look like?"

"He was short and fat?"

"Bingo." Ben returned the money clip to his pocket. "And son?"

"Yes, sir?"

"You have a nice day."

Chapter Nineteen

Claire stepped out of the shower and reached for the towel that was folded and lying on the vanity. She paused for a second, thinking she heard the front door. She stood motionless, listening for another sound. She wondered if she had locked the door. Satisfied that she had imagined it, she dried off, put on her robe, and walked out of the bathroom into her bedroom.

The floor creaked somewhere below, and Claire walked to her bedroom door and opened it. Looking out into the hallway, she called out, "Hello?" She walked into the hall and peered over the railing at the front door, it was closed. "Hello ... is somebody there?"

She made her way down the hall to the top of the stairs and started down. As she walked by the front door she reached over and turned the deadbolt. She went into the living room and looked out the front window. *Why so paranoid?* she thought, shaking her head and grinning to herself.

She walked back into the hallway. Two men stood in the dining room, staring down the hall at her. "Oh my God!" she cried, and backed toward the door.

The larger man put up his hand. "Mrs. Dunning?" he said.

Claire stopped when her back touched the door. She reached down and unlocked it. "Yes," she said nervously.

"I'm Marco Gannon. This is Mr. Petrelli. We didn't mean to startle you. The door was unlocked." He extended his hand toward her.

Claire pulled her robe tight around her neck. "What do you want?"

Petrelli said nothing.

"We were wondering if we could speak with *Mr.* Dunning." Gannon said.

"He's not here."

"The van is in the driveway."

Claire swallowed hard. "He took his truck."

Gannon took a step toward her, and she squeezed her robe tighter. "What time are you expecting him back?"

"I don't know. What is this about?"

Petrelli spoke for the first time. "It's business, Mrs. Dunning." He pulled a business card from his inside jacket pocket. "Here's my card, Mrs. Dunning. Please have him give me a call when he gets home."

Claire took the card and placed it in the pocket of her robe, opened the door, and stepped aside.

"You have a nice day, Mrs. Dunning," Petrelli said as he walked past her.

Gannon paused on his way out. He stared into Claire's eyes and then looked her up and down, taking in every inch. "Be sure and lock the door after we leave, Claire. You can't be too careful these days. There's no telling what a bad man might do to a woman like you if he were to gain access to your home and you were"—He brazenly ogled her again—"barely dressed."

Claire pushed the door closed and locked it when they were gone. She exhaled and wondered if she had been holding her breath the entire time.

Chapter Twenty

Ben put on his blinker as he approached Exit 32.

"Why are we getting off here?" Maggie asked. "Dorchester is Exit 15."

"I need to check on something first," Ben responded.

Maggie scooted closer to the door. "You're not some crazy rapist or something, are you?"

"I'm not sure, but I don't think so," Ben answered matter-of-factly. "If I *were* a rapist, I would have kept your boyfriend's gun and then pulled off the highway into a secluded wooded area where no one would have ever found your body."

"Oh. Now I feel safer."

Ben took a right onto Oakland Street and then a quick left on Garden Street. He read the house numbers as he drove. "Here we are," he said.

"*Where* are we?" Maggie asked.

"I'm not sure."

Ben grabbed his backpack, climbed out of the truck, and looked around before slamming the door. As he walked around the front of the truck Maggie rolled down her window. "Should I just wait here?" she asked.

"I don't care," Ben replied, walking up the brick walkway to the front porch.

Maggie shrugged her shoulders and slumped down in the seat. "I'll just wait here then," she whispered to herself.

Ben walked up the steps and knocked on the front door. He waited for a few seconds and knocked again. No one answered so he side stepped to the front window. Shading his eyes from the light, he peeked in.

"Hey there, what are you doing?" someone hollered from the house next door.

Startled, Ben quickly turned. "I, uh—"

The neighbor started down his steps. "Oh, it's you, Wes. Don't tell me you locked yourself out again," the man said with a chuckle. He was a short, portly man in his early fifties, with brown, thinning hair, and he waddled slightly from side to side when he walked. The waistline of his dark blue jeans was as big around as it was long. His cheeks were bright red. He looked like the poster boy for the warning signs of a stroke.

"Uh, yeah. Lost my damn keys again," Ben answered, trying to hide his confusion.

"You'd lose your head if it wasn't screwed on," the neighbor joked. "I guess that's why you gave me an extra set of keys."

Ben walked off the porch. "Yeah, you know me," he agreed.

"I'll run back in and grab 'em. I'll get your mail for ya, too."

"Thanks … pal."

When Ben's neighbor had gone back inside, Ben shot Maggie a look and shrugged. A few seconds later the man returned. He had a set of keys dangling from his index finger, and in his arms was a cardboard box.

"Here ya go, Wes, your house keys and six months' worth of mail. I didn't realize you would be gone that long when ya asked me to watch the place."

Ben took the keys and box from the man. "I didn't either. One thing led to another and I just couldn't get away."

"I know how that goes." The man looked over toward the truck. "Who's your friend?"

Maggie gave the man a quick glance and a fake smile.

"That's Maggie," said Ben, wondering how much longer he could maintain this farce.

The man walked toward the truck and put out his hand.

"Maggie, this here is … my neighbor … and good friend, uh—"

"Name's Arnold, miss, but my friends call me Slim."

Maggie took his hand and gave it a shake. "Slim?"

Slim chuckled. "Ya know, 'cause I'm not. Like when people call a really tall guy Shorty."

"Yeah, I get it," Maggie replied. "Nice to meet you."

"Likewise, Maggie." Slim turned his attention back to Ben. "I'll catch up with you later, Wes. You can tell me all about your business trip. Six months in the Bahamas! I bet ya got some good stories to tell."

"You have no idea, Slim."

Slim waddled back to his yard, up his steps, and disappeared into the house. Maggie climbed out of the truck and joined Ben at the front door.

Ben tried the first key. It slid into the lock but wouldn't turn. The second key didn't even fit.

"You need some help there?" Maggie asked.

"No." Ben tried the third key, turned it and pushed open the door. "Third time's the charm."

Chapter Twenty-One

Claire slung her pocketbook over her shoulder, turned, and locked the door of the bed and breakfast. On her way across the front yard she glanced down at the brand new tire that looked so out of place on such an old minivan. She knew the other three tires would surely need to be replaced before winter, but she also knew that three more brand new tires would probably cost more than the van was worth.

She climbed into the van and started the engine, but before backing out, she inspected the scraping job that had been put on hold for the time being. *He's doing a nice job*, she thought. It had only been a few hours and Claire missed Ben already. She hoped he wouldn't be gone long.

Knock, knock!

Claire was startled and jumped at the sound of someone rapping on the passenger side window. It was Marvin. She pressed a button on the arm rest and the window lowered.

"He going to scrape today?" Marvin asked.

"Ben's gone out of town for a couple of days, Marv."

"Where'd he go?"

"Boston."

"For what?"

"Business."

"What kind of business?"

Claire thought for a second. "Some paperwork at his old job or something."

Marvin looked suspicious. "I thought he was from the Mid-west."

"His old company has an office in Boston."

Marvin pushed himself away from the van. "Okey doke. Maybe I'll work on it a little bit today, if I get bored."

"You don't have to do that, Marv."

"I know I don't have to. That's the beauty of getting to be my age, Claire. You don't *have* to do anything … or you can do whatever you damn well please."

Claire smiled. "Thanks, Marvin." She rolled up the window, backed out of the driveway, and headed up Shore Drive toward Main Street.

Claire felt bad about lying to Marvin. But what was the flipside, telling him the truth? She didn't know herself what *most* of the truth was. Not even Ben knew exactly who he was. Claire hoped Ben would learn the answer to that question quickly and return to her and Mica. And when he did return, she hoped he would be able to explain it all to her.

Claire hung a left onto Main Street and then turned into Lenny's Garage. She ran over the thin black air hose as she pulled up to the pumps and heard the ding come from inside the office that let Artie know she was there.

Artie walked out of the office and smiled when he saw it was Claire. "I see he got the new tire on for ya."

"Yup. Now I just need three more," Claire answered.

Artie looked the van up and down. "What ya need is a new vehicle."

"My thoughts exactly."

"What can I do for ya?"

"Fill 'er up, Artie, and could you check my washer fluid? The light came on yesterday."

Artie pulled the nozzle from the pump with one hand as he unscrewed the gas cap with the other. "Sure thing." He pulled the lever and braced it in the "on" position as Claire popped the hood.

Artie lifted the hood, looked around, and then went into the garage to get the washer fluid.

"Was it empty?" Claire asked through the window when he returned.

"Yep."

"Good. I figured it was broken or something."

Artie filled the reservoir, put the cap back on, and slammed the hood just as the gas pump clicked off. "Here's the rest of the fluid," he said, handing the jug through the window.

"You would think they'd make the tank hold a whole gallon."

"That's the Canadians for ya. Damn metric system."

Claire tossed the jug into the back seat. "Artie, remember those two guys that were here in the Lincoln yesterday?"

"Yeah. What about 'em?"

"I'm pretty sure I know the answer, but what were they trying to sell you?"

"Security cameras, alarm system, stuff like that. Why do you ask?"

"Ben said they gave an estimate to Howard and Lita for a security system at the bakery."

"Yep, that's what Howard told me at breakfast this morning," Artie said, pointing across the street at the White Rose Diner.

"They seem to be everywhere all of a sudden. They just seem a little shady to me."

Artie laughed. "Ambition ain't a crime, Claire."

"Yeah, that's pretty much what Chet said, too. But I'd bet dollars to donuts those two aren't at the top of the Better Business Bureau's honor roll."

Chapter Twenty-Two

"What exactly are you looking for?" Maggie asked.

Ben stood in the dining room in front of a four-foot oak file cabinet. The top drawer was open, and he was reading the tabs of the file folders as he went through them. "I don't know."

"Then how will you know if you find it?"

Ben slammed the drawer shut. "I don't know!" he hollered.

Maggie jumped. "Sorry. I just thought if I knew what you were looking for then maybe I could help you look."

Ben leaned his forearms against the top of the cabinet and sighed. "These files just contain household bills, repairs, receipts … things that would be in any *normal* person's file cabinet."

"Maybe because you're a *normal* person."

Ben walked back into the living room and looked around. Nothing looked out of place, nothing looked suspicious. The house was neat and well kept. It appeared as though the hardwood floors in the living room and dining room had been recently installed. The walls in the two rooms were painted antique white. The kitchen walls were wallpapered and the original oak moldings throughout the home had, at some point, been stripped and refinished. Ben wondered if he had done this work himself or hired it out.

Ben looked out the living room window. Slim was in his driveway. The hood was up on his car, a red, late-model Chevy Impala, and he was bent over the engine. Ben glanced back at Maggie and said, "You really want to help?"

"I guess."

"Go outside and talk to Slim. Tell him I'm in the shower or something. Pick his brain."

"What do you mean, pick his brain?"

"Ask him questions. Like, how long have I lived here, how long have he and I been friends. Ask him things I might not have told a new girlfriend yet."

"So now I'm your girlfriend?"

"As far as he's concerned."

Maggie looked confused. "How is it you don't already know the answers to these questions?"

"It's a long story, and I don't have time to get into it right now. You just have to trust me."

"Okay, okay. I guess I owe you for rescuing me from Carl." Maggie opened the door and looked back. "Do you want me to ask him what you do for a living?"

"If you were my girlfriend you would already know what I did for a living. Just get him to talk about my job without getting him suspicious."

"I think I can do that," Maggie said as she went out the door.

Ben jogged up the stairs of the two bedroom, one bathroom home. The bathroom was at the top of the stairs. Ben looked inside. Nothing special. The room was in good shape, with outdated fixtures like an antique claw footed tub with a shower ring and curtain, and a wall-mounted porcelain sink. No remodeling had been done to the bathroom, but whoever lived here in the years before Ben had taken great care of everything.

He turned and went into the first bedroom, which contained a twin bed, a wardrobe, a desk, and computer, then down the hall to the master bedroom. Both bedrooms had been remodeled with new sheetrock, paint, ceiling tiles, and carpeting. One wall in the master bedroom was paneled. The old oak molding had been refinished just like the rooms downstairs.

Ben glanced down at the baseboard and noticed that it had been patched at some point. A new piece of oak had been added to extend the baseboard. He looked across at the opposite wall; it had the same patch job.

This was a three bedroom at one time, Ben thought, *and someone moved the wall and turned it into a two bedroom*. He counted the ceiling blocks: fourteen. He went into the spare room and counted: twelve. He then counted the hall and bathroom: thirty-two all together. *There's six feet missing.*

Ben returned to the paneled wall in the master bedroom and rapped on it with his knuckles. When he was almost to the midway point in the wall, the knocking began to sound hollow. Ben pushed on the wall. It moved inward slightly, clicked, and popped open just enough for him to grab it with his fingertips and pull. *A hidden room.*

Ben stepped inside and yanked a pull chain that hung from a bare bulb fixture in the ceiling. The cramped space flooded with light. The room was a little less than six feet wide and ran the full length of the bedroom, about twelve feet. At one end was a gun cabinet with a glass door. Sitting next to the gun cabinet was a large floor safe. At the other end of the room was a small desk with a computer. On the wall above the desk was a large bulletin board. Next to the desk was a file cabinet similar to the one in the dining room. He walked to the desk and flipped on a wall switch. A small track light on the ceiling lit up the bulletin board. Ben scanned the papers, pictures, and receipts pinned to the board. *I wonder what all this stuff means.*

Kneeling down, he opened each of the three drawers in the desk, one at a time, and searched through each. One drawer contained maps and train and subway schedules. Another drawer was filled with large manila envelopes. On each envelope was written a different name, in black marker. Inside each envelope were a driver's license, birth certificate, passport, and credit cards that coincided with each name. Ben's picture was on each license and each passport. He closed the envelopes and then the drawer. The last drawer contained only a black Smith and Wesson 9mm. He picked it up and ejected the magazine, saw that it was fully loaded, and jammed the clip back into the grip. He slid the pistol into the back of his waistband.

He opened each drawer of the file cabinet, glanced in, and then shut them. *It's going to take forever to go through all of this shit.* He shut off the track light and walked to the safe, leaned over, and spun the dial. *How am I ever going to get into this thing?*

The front door opened and then closed. Ben stepped out of the hidden room and pushed the paneled door shut.

"Ben!" Maggie called out.

"Up here!" Ben yelled back.

When Ben got to the bottom of the stairs he glanced out the window, Slims car was gone. Then he turned and saw Maggie walking out of the kitchen with two open bottles of beer.

"Michelob Ultra," Maggie announced, hoisting the beers in the air. "Are you sure you don't live here with a woman?"

"Funny," Ben answered, grabbing one of the bottles. "Anything to eat in that kitchen?"

"If you like spoiled milk and moldy bread. There's a few cans of soup in the cupboard but that's about it. You must eat out a lot."

Ben took a swig of his beer. "Huh, you learn something new every day."

Maggie sat down on the couch. "Did you learn anything new upstairs?"

"Nope. Did you learn anything from my old buddy Slim?" Ben sat down in a chair across from the couch.

"I learned that you have lived here for ten years, and that Slim moved into his house the summer after you. Slim is a self-employed contractor, and he does most of the work on your house. He did the floors in the living room and dining room six months ago while you were away, and you haven't paid him yet."

"Shit, I wonder if there is a checkbook here somewhere." Ben picked up the remote control off of the end table, pointed it at the TV, and pressed the power button. After a few seconds a notice appeared on the screen, THIS CABLE BOX IS NOT AUTHORIZED FOR USE. "Crap! They shut off my cable."

Maggie sipped her beer. "Looks like you don't pay any of your bills."

"The lights are still on."

"The payment must automatically come out of a checking account or off of a credit card each month."

"You're a pretty smart cookie," Ben observed as he shut off the television. "Anything else from Slim?"

"Yes. Evidently you sell insurance."

A deep pucker appeared between Ben's eyebrows. "Insurance?"

"You look disappointed."

"I thought it would be something ... cooler."

Maggie laughed. "If it helps any, you work for a company in Boston, and you specialize in liability insurance for resorts and larger hotels, both foreign and domestic, so you travel a lot."

"Did he give you the name of the company?"

"New England Global."

"That's somewhere to start, I guess," Ben said as he stood. "Come on, I better get you home. I can come back and look through this stuff later."

"Can we get something to eat first? I'm starving."

"We can do that. It'll give you a chance to fill me in on who your boyfriend is and why he's got such a high opinion of himself. And more importantly, what a smart girl like you is doing with a douche bag like Carl in the first place."

"Okay, but only if you explain to me why you're searching through your own house, and why you don't seem to know a neighbor you've lived next to for almost ten years, and why he called you Wes but you call yourself Ben."

Ben gulped down the last of his beer and sat the bottle on the table. "Sounds like a plan," he said and grabbed his backpack as he stood up. He unzipped the top, pulled the gun from his waistband, and shoved it inside.

Maggie's eyes focused on the gun. "What's that for?"

"You never know."

Chapter Twenty-Three

"Mom!" Mica called out as he shot like a bullet through the front door. "Mom!

Claire was in the basement and couldn't hear her son, but she heard the door slam and his feet as they pounded down the hall and across the dining room. She slammed the dryer door, turned a knob, and pushed a button.

Mica stood at the top of the basement stairs. "Mom, are you down there?"

"Ye-*es*," Claire hollered back. "I'll be right up."

When Claire got to the kitchen, Mica had the lid off of the cookie jar. "Empty," he informed her.

"No kidding. It's not a bottomless jar, you know. There were two left, and Ben took them with him."

Mica replaced the lid and frowned. "Did you hear from him?"

"Not yet."

"Do you think he might come home tonight?"

"Probably not. He said it might be a couple of days."

"So, tomorrow then?"

"I don't know, Mica. He said he had a few things to take care of, and then he would be home."

"What kind of things?"

"Jesus, you sound like Marvin. Just things."

"Okay, okay. What's for dinner?"

"I thought we'd eat at The Cove tonight. Why don't you go and get started on your homework. I'm waiting for guests to arrive, and once they get settled in, we'll head downtown."

"Okay." Mica walked back into the dining room, picked up his book bag, and tossed it on the table.

"The guests will be here any minute, so why don't you take your homework upstairs to your room and do it."

Mica rolled his eyes. "Whatever."

"Don't whatever me," Claire scolded.

"Sorry." He picked up the bag and went down the hall. When he got to the stairs, he heard a thud and looked out the window. Marvin was maneuvering his ladder into place and had bumped the siding.

"Mom!"

"Yeah?"

"Mr. Polinowski is out front. He's going to scrape paint. Can I go out and help him and do my homework later when we get home?"

Claire would rather Mica just went up and did his homework, but she would also rather Marvin wasn't working on the house by himself. "Go ahead!" she called out.

"Yes!" Mica ran up the stairs as fast as he could, opened his bedroom door, and threw his book bag on his bed. In a flash he had sprinted back down the stairs to the front porch.

"Mr. Polinowski, my mom said I could help you scrape the house."

"She did, did she? There's another scraper lying right there on the ground. Why don't you grab that small step ladder over there and start doing the trim around the front door."

Mica jumped off the porch and grabbed the scraper. "What should I do after the door?"

Marvin snickered at Mica's eagerness. "One step at a time, boy, one step at a time."

Mica and Marvin had only scraped for about half an hour when a black Suburban pulled into the driveway. A man and a woman in their mid to late fifties climbed from the vehicle.

"Good afternoon," the man said.

Marvin tried to be more polite than usual, knowing these were probably guests of Claire's. "Good afternoon to you, sir," he said.

"I'm Jim Reagan, and this is my wife Judy."

"Nice to meet you. I'm Marvin Polinowski. I live next door."

Mica spoke up. "I'm Mica. My mom owns The Colsome House Bed and Breakfast." He pointed toward the door. "You can go right in here to register, and after you bring in your bags you can park out back."

"Well, thank you, young man," Judy said.

"You're welcome." Mica stepped back from the door and let the couple pass.

Jim paused at the door and held out his car keys. "Son, if you grab our luggage from the back of the truck and take it up to our room, there's five bucks in it for you."

Mica snatched the keys. "Thanks, mister!"

"Ya hired my man right out from underneath me," Marvin joked.

Chapter Twenty-Four

"That's some story," Maggie said as she mopped up the ketchup on her plate with her last French fry. "Amnesia … weird. I thought that only happened in sitcoms and soap operas."

Ben tipped up his pint glass and poured the last of his Guinness down his throat. He had told Maggie his story—not his whole story of course, just the part about the car accident. He told her the part about having lost his memory, and about living with Claire and Mica. He changed their names in his tale, and when Maggie asked him the name of the town where he had been living he side-stepped the question, not wanting her to know too much about him.

"It's weird all right," said Ben. "Shall we get out of here?"

"Sure," Maggie replied, wiping her mouth with her napkin.

They left the pub, got back on I-93, and resumed the half hour trip to Maggie's mother's house in Dorchester.

"So," Ben asked, "how did you ever get mixed up with a guy like Carl Bianchi?"

"Carl's not such a bad guy," Maggie answered.

"You said his family is in organized crime. I bet that's not the first time he's slapped you around, and you're telling me he's not a bad guy? That's the definition of 'bad guy.'"

Maggie stared out the window at the road ahead. "I know … you're right. It's just that … he's good to me."

"Except when he's not."

"You wouldn't understand."

"That's something we can agree on."

"My exit is right up here," Maggie said, as she pointed at the exit sign.

Ben flipped on his blinker, got off at Exit 15, and took a right onto Columbia Road. When he came to the corner of Bowdoin Street and Geneva Avenue, he pulled into the Walgreens parking lot.

"Why are we stopping here?" Maggie asked.

"I have to grab something quick," Ben replied, climbing from the truck. "Wait here."

"Yes, sir," Maggie joked and saluted. "Lambskin or latex—makes me no never mind."

"Very funny."

Ben walked through the automatic doors and looked around.

"Can I help you?" said a young, pale-skinned, freckle-faced redhead. He wore a white shirt with a button down collar, a wide blue clip-on tie, and a name tag that read, WALGREENS— BRENT, ASSISTANT MANAGER. He was eager to please and Ben didn't want to disappoint him.

"Where do you hide your cell phones?" Ben asked.

"Aisle four, sir."

"Thank you," Ben remarked as he walked past the young man.

Ben grabbed the cheapest pre-paid flip-phone on the rack, along with a car charger, paid for them with cash, and returned to the truck.

"That was quick," Maggie observed.

Ben tossed the bag onto the seat and climbed in. "Needed a new cell phone." He opened the package and began reading the instructions.

Maggie pulled the phone from the package and looked it over, and then she opened the charger and plugged it in to the cigarette lighter. She took the prepaid card out of the package and then flipped open the phone and began pressing buttons.

Ben read the instructions to himself all the while sporting a confused expression. He scratched his head and began reading from the beginning again. Maggie spoke into the phone; Ben ignored her.

"These instructions might as well be written in Chinese," Ben said and tossed the pamphlet on the truck seat.

"That's just because you're old," Maggie replied, and pushed a few more buttons. "Here you go, all set."

Ben took the phone. "What's my phone number?"

"I saved it in your contacts under 'Me'."

"How do I find my contacts?"

Maggie rolled her eyes. "Maybe you need a Playskool toy phone first and then work up to the real thing."

"Cut the comedy. Now, how do I find my contacts?"

"Press the little button under the picture of the phone book."

Ben complied; the only contact was Me. "Cool," he said.

"Do you need me to dial it for you?"

"No, smartass." Ben dialed the phone.

"Hello?"

"Hey, it's me."

Claire's voice registered delight and relief. "Oh, hi! How's everything going?"

"Good. How's everything going there?"

Claire thought about telling Ben about her unexpected guests that morning, but thought it might worry him. She knew he already had enough on his mind and decided to wait until he returned. "Fine. I miss you."

"Already? I've only been gone for eight hours."

"I guess I'm just used to you always being here. I love you."

"I love you too," Ben said quietly.

Maggie rolled her eyes and started making loud kissing noises. Ben shot her a look and she stopped.

"What was that?" Claire asked.

"Nothing," Ben replied. "Did this number come up on the caller ID?"

"Yes."

Put it in your cell phone, it's my new number."

"I will."

"What's for dinner?" Ben asked, missing home.

"I thought Mica and I would head down to The Cove for dinner."

"Well, I better get going. I'll call you later. I love you."

"You too," Claire responded and hung up.

"Well, that was sweet," Maggie said.

"Tell me something, Maggie, do you always have to be a sarcastic bitch?"

"I was being serious! Carl would never tell me he loved me in a million years."

"And yet he's not such a bad guy—your words."

Maggie looked down at her lap. "My words."

Smart, pretty girl like you could do a lot better than being a greasy gangster's moll."

Maggie looked up, her eyes snapping fire. "Wanna ditch the armchair psychoanalysis and get me the hell home now?"

The hum of the road was the only sound they heard for the rest of the trip.

Chapter Twenty-Five

Claire retrieved her cell from her purse and programmed in Ben's cell number. When she opened the front door, Mica was scraping around the living room window.

"Mica, why don't you come in and get cleaned up and change your clothes? We'll go get something to eat," She suggested, stepping out onto the porch. "Marvin, would you like to join Mica and me for dinner at The Cove? It's on me … for all your help."

Marvin pulled up his shirt sleeve and looked at his watch. "You don't have to do that, Claire," he said. "I was going to head in in a bit and make myself a can of soup or something."

Claire smiled. "I know I don't *have* to, Marvin. I don't *have* to do anything. I *want* to."

Marvin chuckled, knowing he had just been given a dose of his own medicine. "Ya got me on that one, Claire." He began picking up his tools and folding the step ladders.

"Can you give me about twenty minutes? I need to take a bath."

Good! You needed one since the moment I met you. "Sure can. Come on, Mica"

When the door slammed behind them, Marvin headed home at a good clip.

*****

Mica ran ahead of his mother and pulled open the door of The Cove restaurant and held it as she and Marvin walked in.

"Thank you, sir," Marvin said as he walked by.

"Good evening, Claire," said Marcia, hunched over a wooden podium next to the door. "Three this evening?"

"Yes, three," Claire responded.

Marvin looked Marcia up and down as she grabbed three menus from inside the podium and stepped out from behind it. "I've never seen you out from behind the bar before, Marcia. I didn't even know you had legs."

Mica laughed and Marvin gave him a wink.

Marcia shot him a disgruntled look. "Yeah, well, Sam's training a new bartender tonight so he stuck me at the door."

Marvin glanced to the bar. "Pretty girl."

"I guess," Marcia replied.

"Well, like they say, out with the old, in with the new," Marvin recited.

"Thanks, Marvin, that helped," she said sarcastically and led them to their table.

The trio sat and Marcia placed a menu in front of each one of them. "You know what you want to drink?"

Mica spoke first. "I'll have a Coke."

Marvin looked to Claire and waited for her to order first. "A glass of Moscato, please," she said.

"And I'll have a Manhattan," Marvin said.

"Coming right up." Marcia strolled over to the bar.

Mica didn't need to open his menu. "I already know what I want."

Marvin scanned *his* menu, disappointed there were no pictures of the grub. "What are ya thinking, boy?"

"The lobster roll and fries."

"You just made up my mind for me," Marvin said, closing his menu.

A short time later Marcia returned with a tray full of drinks. "Here ya go," she said as she set their drinks in front of them. "Have you decided what to order?"

"Me and Marvin are having the lobster-roll," Mica blurted out.

"Good choice! And for you, Claire?"

"I'm going to get that chicken special on the board up there."

"The Chicken Piccata?"

"That's the one."

Marcia scribbled the orders on her pad and said, "I'll put these right in. If ya need anything else, just give a holler."

"Wait just a minute, Marcia," Mica spoke up. "Can we get an appetizer, Mom?"

"Appetizer or dessert," Claire said. "You decide. You can't have both."

Marcia stuck her pencil behind her ear. "You may want to pick the dessert. We have apple pie a la mode tonight."

Mica looked confused. "What's al a mode?"

Marvin took a big sip of his drink. "That's how the Frenchies say *with ice cream*."

Mica looked to Claire. "Really, Mom?"

"For the most part."

"That's awesome!" Mica said, unwrapping his straw and jamming it into his soda. "Is it too late to order the lobster roll al a mode?"

"I'll see what I can do," Marcia answered, laughing, and headed back to the kitchen.

Marvin downed the last of his Manhattan. "I'm gonna walk up to the bar, Claire, and order myself another drink."

Claire nodded and Marvin got up from the table. When he reached the bar he slid his empty glass forward. To his right sat Curt Holliday, and to his left was Artie Legg, still dressed in his gray coveralls from the garage. The bartender stood at the other end of the bar, her nose in her cell phone, fingers flitting over the buttons at blinding speed.

"Marv," Curt said.

"Curt," Marvin answered.

"Marv," Artie said.

"Artie," Marvin replied. He reached out, picked up his glass, and shook the ice in an attempt to get the bartenders attention.

Curt jerked his head toward the good looking young girl behind the bar. "What do you think of the new bartender, Marv?"

"I think she's young enough to be your daughter, Curt."

Curt gave the old geezer's bony shoulder a squeeze. "Every woman is young enough to be someone's daughter, Marv."

Marvin tapped his glass on the bar a couple times. "You might want to keep that in mind while you sit here ogling her, ya sick bastard."

Curt took a sip of his beer. "Anyone ever tell you you're a real prick, Marv?"

"If I only had a dollar, Curt, if I only had a dollar."

The young girl smiled as she read her text message.

"Miss?" Marvin called out.

She looked irritated when she glanced up from her phone. "Hold on," she said.

"You take your time, Princess, we got all day," Curt said.

Marvin shot him a look. "I ain't got all day."

Artie remained silent, but grinned as he stared into the bottom of his beer mug.

"She's texting," Curt said. "That's what the kids do nowadays. Back in your day I guess the fad was drawing on cave walls with charcoal, huh?"

"Good one, Curt," said Artie

Marvin twitched his beetling brows in annoyance. "She's supposed to be *working*," he replied, loud enough for Princess to hear him.

She placed her phone on the bar and walked over to Marvin in slow motion. "What do you need?"

"Another Manhattan."

"I don't know how to make that."

"Then why are you here?" Marvin asked.

"Because my uncle said I needed to get a job. *God!*"

Marvin held up his glass. "Who made this one?"

The young girl nodded her head toward Marcia, who was waiting on another table. "Her."

Marvin snatched up his glass. "Let me show you how," he said, and made his way around behind the bar.

"I don't think you should be back here," she said snottily.

"Well you probably shouldn't be back here either, *Princess*." Marvin scooped some ice into his glass, grabbed a bottle of whiskey out of the well, and added a shot.

"What the hell are you doing behind the bar, Marv?" came a brusque voice. It was Sam O'Brien, the owner of The Cove. Sam stood in the kitchen doorway, his foot propping open the door, his catcher's mitt hands wrapped around each doorjamb.

"Making a drink, Sammy. What does it look like I'm doing?"

Sam was just a few inches under seven feet tall. His biceps were the size of hams, which was unusual for a sixty-five year old man. His silver hair was combed straight back. He wore a black T-shirt that was one size too small. Sam denied it, but everyone in town knew that his year round dark tan came from the local tanning salon. "It looks like you're standing behind *my* bar," he said.

"Maybe because *your* new bartender can't get off of her damn phone long enough to make *your* customers a drink." Marvin tipped up the bottle of vermouth, replaced it on the shelf behind him, and started back around the bar.

"I told you to leave your phone in the car, Lily," Sam said.

"But what if I get a call?"

"If it's an emergency, they'll call the restaurant."

"We'll see what my uncle has to say about this." Lily returned to the other end of the bar to retrieve her cell phone. "I'm going on break."

"I thought she *was* on break," Marvin joked.

Lily turned up her nose. "Very funny."

Curt watched Lily's ass as she walked across the dining room and out the front door. "Where did you find her?" he asked.

"Oh, I hired her as a favor to the guy that installed some security lights and cameras for me. Starting to regret it."

"The guys that are leaving the flyers around town?" Artie asked.

"Yeah, those guys," Sam answered.

"They stopped by my place too," Artie commented. "Seemed friendly at first, but when I told them I wasn't interested, they got a little pushy."

"Claire said they came to her place this morning looking for Ben. Scared the hell out of her," Marvin interjected.

"Where is Ben?" Curt asked.

"Went into Boston for something," Marvin answered.

Curt looked past Marvin to Artie. "Did you tell Marv about the flat tire?"

Artie gave him the old why-don't-you-keep-your-big-mouth-shut look and then glanced over his shoulder at Claire. "Not so loud," he ordered.

Marvin also looked back at Claire and then whispered, "Why, what's up?"

"Ben brought in a flat tire the other morning," Artie said.

"Yeah, so?" Marvin responded.

"When I took the tire off of the rim there was a small round piece of pointed metal inside, like someone had poked a hole in the tire on purpose, with an ice pick or something, and broke off the handle."

"I wonder what kind of a dick would do a thing like that?" Sam asked.

"Been some other strange things happen lately too," Curt said. "Sign got smashed over to the hardware store, and Howard said he caught someone snoopin' around out in the alley behind his store."

"A window got smashed over to Lucy's Diner too," Artie added.

"Huh," Marv let out. "Let's not say anything about the tire to Claire. No need to worry her. I'll tell Ben about it when he gets back."

"When's he supposed to be back?" Sam asked.

"Not sure," Marvin answered. "Soon, I hope."

Chapter Twenty-Six

Ben pulled his truck to the curb in front of a large white Victorian that sat behind a four-foot chain link fence.

Maggie quickly leaned over and kissed him on the cheek. "Well, thanks for the ride."

Ben put the truck in park. "No problem. I'll wait here till you get inside."

"Do you want to come in?"

"No, I better get back to Medford. Have a lot of paperwork and other things to go through tonight. I would like to get back home early tomorrow."

"And where exactly is home?"

"Probably best if you didn't know that."

"Suit yourself," Maggie said and jumped out of the truck. "I have your cell number if I need you to rescue me again."

"Let's hope I don't have to."

Maggie smiled and winked. "Have a nice life." She slammed the door.

Ben watched as she went through the gate and up the red brick walkway that led to the front porch. When Maggie got to the storm door she opened it, turned, gave Ben one of those peculiarly feminine waves that involved jiggling the fingers ridiculously, and went inside. Ben put the car in drive and pulled away from the curb.

When he got to the end of Bloomfield Street, he turned right onto Geneva and immediately pulled to the curb. Pulling the map from the dashboard, he attempted to plot his path out of Dorchester and back onto the highway. He ran his finger over the crumpled map searching for Bloomfield or Geneva. He heard the sound of skateboard wheels on the blacktop and looked out the window.

"Hey, kid!" Ben called out to the teenage boy rolling toward him.

"Yeah?"

"Can you tell me how to get back onto 93?"

The boy stomped on the end of his board and caught it in midair. "Sure, just go right to the end of this road and turn right, then go up a few streets and take a left."

Ben searched the map as the boy spoke. "What street do I take a left on?" he asked, and then his cell phone rang. "Hold on."

"I ain't got all day, mister."

Ben rolled his eyes and answered the phone. "Hello?"

"Wes?"

He paused for a second. "Yes."

"Hey, it's Maggie."

"Everything okay?" Ben asked.

"Sure, everything is fine, Wes. I was just wondering if you could swing back by quick. My mother wanted to thank you for helping me out today."

"That's not necessary, Maggie."

"Come on, Wes, she just wanted to meet you."

Ben thought for a few seconds. Something didn't smell right; there was a false note in Maggie's voice.

"Wes, are you there?"

"Yeah, Maggie. I was just about to get back on the highway. I'll turn around. I need to stop and get some gas, so give me about twenty-five minutes or so."

"Okay, Wes, thanks."

Ben hung up his cell and glanced back over at the boy. "Take a right up here," the kid repeated.

"Never mind. Thanks any way, kid." Ben tossed the map into the passenger seat and drove down the street, taking the next right. As he drove along Tonawanda Street, he looked through each yard at the back of the houses on Bloomfield. When he saw the rear of the white Victorian, he pulled to the curb and parked. When he climbed from the truck he leaned back inside, grabbed his pack, unzipped it, pulled out the pistol, and jammed it in his waistband. It felt comfortable, like it belonged there.

Ben ran down the driveway of a house that looked very much like the one he was headed for. Many of the houses in the neighborhood were similar. This one was green with white trim and a small garage sat at the end of the driveway. Ben ran between the garage and a six-foot stockade fence.

When he came to the end of the yard he put his foot on the bottom rail of the fence and pushed himself up and over, landing on his feet and quickly dropping to his knees in Maggie's mother's backyard. Her home also had a garage, and Ben ran to the back of it to keep out of view of anyone in the house.

Ben scanned the back of the house. There was an old wooden back door, probably leading to the kitchen, he assumed. A set of four steps led to the door; there was no back porch. The door had a glass insert, and anyone in the kitchen would be able to see him running up the steps. *Better make this as quick and efficient as possible*, he thought.

Yanking the gun from his pants he ran as fast as he could toward the back door. His left foot hit the second step, his right hit the top step, and he threw his shoulder into the door, shattering the jamb and glass. The door swung violently open. Ben landed on his back on the kitchen floor and in one fluid motion rolled to his knee.

A man standing in the doorway between the kitchen and dining room reached for the weapon stored in his shoulder holster. Before the pistol cleared the holster, Ben had fired two shots, the first in the man's cheek and the second found his forehead.

Ben was to his feet and running toward the man before the thug even realized he was dead. With his left hand, Ben grabbed the man's gun from his holster as he fell.

Ben heard the sound of someone upstairs running, and out of the corner of his eye he saw a figure to his right. He dove through the doorway into the dining room, firing his weapon four times, as he flew through the air, into the chest of a man who had turned toward him after looking out a window on the side of the house. The impact of the bullets drove the goon backwards into the window.

Ben hit the dining room floor on his back just as a third man was running down the stairs. Ben fired twice, once from each weapon. Struck once in the abdomen and once in the throat, the man tumbled down the stairs.

The house was silent; no movement. "Maggie!" he called out.

He waited … nothing … nothing … a floorboard above him creaked.

Ben rolled to his knees and jumped to his feet. He slowly and cautiously made his way up the stairs. When his eyes reached the second level, Ben could see into a bedroom. An elderly woman sat on the floor, her back against the open door. Tears ran down her cheeks. She pointed toward the bathroom at the top of the stairs. Ben shook his head yes and put a silencing finger to his lips and motioned with his flattened palm for her to stay put.

Ben waited on the stairs. "Carl!" he called out. There was no answer, but he could hear the muffled sounds of Maggie sobbing. "Carl, your men are all dead. You're all alone."

"There's more men on the way," Carl called back. "You're a dead man."

Ben looked around the hall. He saw a broom leaning against the wall and grabbed it. "That just means I have to kill you sooner."

Ben advanced up the stairs. The bathroom door was open a few inches. He could just make out Maggie's bloody and bruised reflection in the mirror over the vanity. She was cowering in a corner of the shower behind a sliver of curtain.

Reaching out with the broom handle, he pushed open the bathroom door. It creaked, and Carl fired a round through the shower curtain.

Ben went up the last few steps. "I'm going to count to ten, Carl, and if you don't toss out your gun, I'm going to kill you."

Carl fired through the curtain again. The two holes were an inch apart.

"One."

Ben inched toward the bathroom door.

"Two."

He slowly reached his arm into the room and gently placed the barrel of his pistol up to one of the bullet holes in the shower curtain.

"Three."

Ben fired three shots through the hole. There was a loud thud as Carl hit the back wall and then fell forward through the curtain, ripping it from the rod, and falling face first to the bathroom tile.

"Ten."

A crimson Rorschach splatter decorated the shower wall where Carl had been. Maggie stood frozen in the corner, her mascara running down her face.

"Can I get you a towel?" Ben joked.

"Where's my mother?" Maggie asked.

"She's fine, she's right here."

Ben held out his hand and Maggie grabbed it, leaping out of the shower and into his arms. "Thank you, Ben," she said.

Maggie's mother had just walked into the hall. She gasped when she saw Carl's body. "Wait," she said, "I thought his name was Wes?"

Ben smiled. "Only when she's in trouble."

The old woman looked confused.

"I'll explain it later, Mom." She turned to Ben. "Thanks for rescuing me—again. As you've probably already figured out, Carl didn't take kindly to me ditching him and came here with his guys for revenge. It was a setup, Ben. He made me call you."

Ben gently pushed Maggie away. "I figured that out. The cops are going to be here any second."

"What are we going to say?"

"We don't have enough time to come up with a *good* story. You'll have to tell them that Carl and his three friends were here, they terrorized you and your mom, then some badass—"

"Badass?" Maggie interrupted, grinning.

"Work with me here, Maggie. Some badass kicked in the back door, there was a lot of gunfire, and the badass escaped out the back door after it was over."

"So, basically tell the truth."

"Yes, only describe a badass that doesn't look like me. Use your imagination—maybe he was from a rival gang."

Ben pulled a hand towel from the towel bar and wiped off the gun he had borrowed from the dead man downstairs. When he finished, he dropped the gun to the floor and returned his to his waistband.

"I gotta go," he said.

"Wait!" Maggie placed her hands on Ben's face and pulled him to her. Ben didn't resist her masterful kiss. "So long, badass. Take care of yourself."

The sirens were blaring when Ben retraced his steps back to his truck, a stupid grin plastered on his face.

Chapter Twenty-Seven

"Well, that was one awesome lobster roll," Marvin reminisced, as Claire brought the minivan to a halt in the driveway. Marvin looked at his watch. "I think I have just enough time to get in a nap before bedtime."

Mica laughed. "Me too."

Claire put the old van in park and shut off the engine. "You have just enough time to get some homework done before bedtime, young man."

"But, Mom, it's Friday."

"That doesn't mean you can't get started on it."

"Fine."

Marvin jumped in with, "And try to get plenty of rest tonight so you can give me a hand on the house tomorrow."

Mica opened his door. "Okay, Mr. Polinowski," he answered and jumped out of the van.

Marvin and Claire opened their doors just as Claire's cell phone went off. She reached in her purse and pulled it out. "Hey, stranger, what's up?"

"Not much. Just checking in," came Ben's voice. "How was dinner?"

"Good. We treated Marv to dinner for all the work he's been doing on the house."

"He's a good man."

Claire glanced over at Marvin who hadn't left the vehicle yet. "Yes he is," she agreed.

"I'm going to stay here tonight and probably head back tomorrow afternoon."

"Okay, I'll see you tomorrow then. I love you."

"I love you too," Ben said and then hung up.

Claire started to put her phone away.

"I've been thinking about getting a cell phone, Claire," Marvin blurted out.

"You have?"

"Don't sound so surprised. I was just thinking it might be a handy thing to have."

"They are handy," Claire agreed.

"Maybe you could help me get it going when I buy it."

"Sure, I can do that, Marv."

Marvin held out his hand. "Can I have a look at yours?"

"Sure," Claire responded, handing him the phone.

Marvin inspected the phone. "Where's the buttons?"

"Press that button on the side there, and the key board lights up."

Marvin pressed it. "Oh yeah, will you look at that! This got that caller ID thing, like the house phone?"

"Yes."

"Is there a way to look back and see who called you—you know, in case you miss the call?"

"Yes." Claire reached over and tapped a couple of icons and the last number appeared.

"That's amazing," Marvin said, staring at the screen. "Well, I better be getting in." Marvin leapt from the van with surprising spryness and quickly hot footed it toward his house.

"You want to come in for a cup of coffee, Marv?" Claire called out.

Marvin ignored the question as he hurried up the steps. His lips were moving rapidly as he talked to himself.

Claire shrugged her shoulders and climbed out of the van.

Marvin slammed his door behind him as he feverishly recited the same numbers over and over to himself. He grabbed his phone and dialed the numbers.

"Hello?" Ben said.

"Ben, it's Marvin."

"Marvin?"

"Your neighbor … Marvin."

"Yeah, I know. Is everything all right?"

"Everything is fine, Ben … I mean Claire and Mica are fine."

"Are you okay, Marv?" Ben asked. He could hear the concern in Marvin's tone."

"Yeah, I'm fine too. It's just … I wanted to give you a call because I talked to Artie tonight at The Cove; he mentioned your flat tire. Ben, he said it looked like someone did it on purpose. He said it looked like someone had jabbed it with an ice pick or something."

"What makes him think it wasn't just a nail?"

"He said a sharp piece of metal had broken off inside the tire," Marvin explained.

"Does Claire know?"

"She didn't hear him and I didn't mention it. I told Artie not to say anything to her about it."

"Thanks, Marv, no need to worry her."

"That's not all, Ben. Those two security guys who been driving around town in that Lincoln showed up at your house this morning, after you had left. Claire said they came right in the house. She was just getting out of the shower. Said it really scared her."

"She didn't say anything to me about it."

"She said *she* didn't want to worry *you*."

"Okay, Marv thanks for calling. Don't tell Claire you called me."

"I know, I know," Marvin said. "You don't want to worry her."

"Do you think you could make up some reason to go over to the house for a while? I have one more stop to make, and then I think I'll go ahead and come home tonight. I would appreciate it if you could just go over and hang around till I get home. Shouldn't be more than an hour and a half."

"Sure will, Ben. She invited me over for coffee when we got home from The Cove. I'll just go back over and tell her I changed my mind."

"Thanks, Marv. I'll see you in a bit."

Marvin said, "Bye," and hung up his phone. He picked up a pencil that was lying next to the phone. He wrote down the first digit of Ben's cell phone number and his mind went blank. "Shit!" he said and tossed the pencil back on the stand.

Chapter Twenty-Eight

Ben hung a right onto Garden Street and pulled to the curb across from his house in Medford. *Home sweet home,* he thought, and climbed out of the truck.

Slim arrived home and swung his old Buick into the driveway. "Where's your pretty little friend, Wes?" he asked.

Ben paused at the sidewalk. "Ran her home to her mothers. What's going on tonight, Slim?"

"Loretta sent me down to the Redbox pick up a couple DVDs. Probably just stay in and watch a movie, I guess."

Ben tried his best to make conversation, and make it sound as though he and Slim had known each other for years. "Anything good?"

Slim oozed his bulk out of the Buick, held up the packages, and read each title. "*Goodfellas* and *Casino*." Slim got out of the car.

"Loretta a big fan of Mob movies?"

"No, but I am," Slim replied. "Whatever the movie is, she'll be up and in the kitchen ten minutes into it, doing the dishes. Then she'll come back in and ask me what's going on. As soon as she gets caught up, she'll be upstairs folding laundry. She usually gets settled in a few minutes before the credits roll with a bunch of pesky questions about the movie."

Ben laughed. "How about a quick beer before you start your movie?"

"Sure, but I'm not drinking that carbonated piss you call beer. Why don't you come over and say hello to Loretta and we'll have a *good* beer?"

Ben agreed and followed Slim to his house.

"Lore!" Slim called out as he waddled through the door. "Look who's here to grace us with his presence."

"I'll be right down!" Loretta hollered. Slim slammed the door behind him.

"Have a seat, Wes. I'll grab those beers."

Ben looked around the room; nothing seemed familiar. Even after six months, he still hoped that something would trigger a lost memory. He took a seat on the couch.

"Here ya go, pal," Slim said, handing Ben an open bottle of Saranac Black Forest.

Ben took a big gulp. "Tasty." He cringed a little as he swallowed the dark beer.

"Only got six left till my brother visits from Utica. I can have him bring you a few cases if you want. He and his wife are supposed to be here in May."

"No, that's okay. I don't know how much I'll be around."

"What do you mean?" Slim asked.

"Might be getting a transfer," Ben lied.

"That's too bad, Wes. We been neighbors a long time."

"I know, Slim, but it's an offer I can't refuse, as they would say in one of your Mob movies."

"Loretta and I will hate to see you go." Slim reached out with his beer and the two men clinked their bottles together. "To new neighbors, hope they're as quiet as you've been."

"Don't get too far ahead of yourself; I probably won't put the house up for sale right away. And that reminds me—what do I owe you for the floors?"

Slim hoisted his pear-shaped body with a primal grunt and started out of the room. "I got your bill made up right in here." He returned a few seconds later and handed Ben two sheets of paper. "One is for the floors and the other is for the secret room upstairs."

Ben's eyes shot quickly to Slim. "The secret room?" he blurted out.

"Yeah, minus the deposit you gave me, of course. That's the price we agreed on."

"So you know about the secret room?"

"Yes," Slim answered hesitantly.

"Why did I tell you I needed a secret room, Slim?"

Slim took another swig of his beer. "I assumed it was because you didn't want that giant safe I got you, and that gun cabinet, sticking out like sore thumbs in the middle of your bedroom."

"Right," Ben agreed.

"Is everything okay, Wes?"

"Not exactly. I forgot the combination to the safe."

"That's no problem, you told me to keep it written down in *my* paperwork." Slim stood again, a little trumpeting fart accompanying the effort. "I'll grab it for you." When he returned, he handed Ben an index card with the combination typed across the center. "Problem solved."

Ben downed the last of his beer. "You're a lifesaver. I better get going." He sat his empty bottle on the coffee table.

"Lore!" Slim bellowed once again. "Wes is here. Get down here and say hello."

Ben heard the stairs creaking with each of Loretta's steps and could hear her heavy breathing as she reached the bottom of the staircase. Loretta was a big woman and reminded Ben a little of Lita, from the bakery. He had a mercifully fleeting fantasy of Slim and Loretta having sex and prayed the giant economy sized couple had earthquake insurance.

Ben pretended he was glad to see Loretta, smiled big, and held out his arms for a hug. He hoped the display wasn't over the top. He soon found out it wasn't.

Loretta threw her arms around Ben and squeezed. "Where have you been? I was beginning think we should call the cops and have 'em put out an APB on your behind."

Ben was still gripped deep in Loretta's hug. He wondered if she had ever wrestled professionally.

"Business just took a little longer than usual," came his muffled voice from somewhere inside the colossal bosom.

Loretta finally released him. "Well, you're home now, and that's what matters." She straightened Ben's shirt.

"But not for long, I'm afraid," Slim cut in. "Wes may be leaving us for greener pastures."

"What?"

Ben put up his hands. "It's nothing definite yet. Let's not get all riled up. We'll just see how it all plays out."

Loretta put her hand on her heart. "We would hate to lose you as a neighbor, Wes."

"I have to get going." He put up his arms. "One more hug for the road."

After the goodbyes were said and Loretta had even shed a tear, Ben asked Slim to walk him out.

When they got out to the sidewalk, Ben turned to Slim. "I just wanted to say thanks for everything you've done for me, and for being a good neighbor and friend these past few years." He held out his hand and Slim gave it a hearty shake.

"You're talking like this is the end, buddy. Just because you might be moving doesn't mean we'll never see each other again."

Ben felt a sadness as he looked into Slim's eyes. It wasn't sadness about leaving; he didn't even really know Slim and Loretta. He figured he was just sad because of the loss he was putting on someone else. It was obvious to him that he meant a lot to his neighbors, and at some point they had probably meant a lot to him. But those days had been forgotten.

As Ben walked up his front steps and to his door he wondered if some day it would all come back to him, and he would feel a sudden urge to come back and see his old friends.

Ben pressed on the bedroom wall and the hidden panel popped open. He flipped on the lights and went directly to the safe. Reading the index card, he spun the dial to the right, to the left, and then back to the right. Turning the handle and pulling, the heavy door opened.

Sitting on a shelf in the center of the safe were nine stacks of bills. In each stack were bills banded together with yellow bands labeled $2000.00. There were about ten of those in each stack.

"Holy shit," Ben whispered. "Screw house painting."

Chapter Twenty-Nine

Jim and Judy Reagan, the B&B's guests, sat on the sofa. Marvin was sitting in the puffy red chair in front of the fireplace, and Claire was seated on the loveseat that sat under the front window. Jim and Marvin sipped their coffee from white mugs. Jim's mug read, STATE FARM and Marvin's said, DUNQUIN COVE, MAINE, with a big red lobster in the center.

Judy and Claire drank their coffee from white teacups with delicate ivy twining around the rim.

I the last half hour, Jim and Judy had just returned from a rehearsal dinner.

"Who's getting married?" Marvin inquired.

"Judy's niece," Jim answered.

"Where's the wedding being held?"

"The Stage Neck Inn," Judy responded.

"Beautiful place," Claire commented.

Judy sat her cup and saucer on the table. "Well, I'd better be off to bed—got a long day ahead of me."

"I'm right behind you, dear," Jim remarked. "A bunch of us guys are playing golf tomorrow morning."

"Will you be here for breakfast?" Claire asked.

"No, we're all meeting at a place called The Lobster Cove for breakfast," Jim answered. He followed Judy up the stairs.

"Looks like it's just you and me for breakfast, Claire," she sang out from the landing.

"I'll save you a seat," Claire joked.

Marvin looked at his watch and then at the clock above the fireplace.

"You've been watching that clock pretty close," Claire pointed out.

"Have I?"

"Yes, you have. What's up?"

"Nothing. I was feeling a little hungry, and I was wondering how long it had been since we ate."

"Can I get you something to eat, Marvin?"

"You mentioned apple pie earlier."

"I did. Would you like some?"

"Maybe just a small piece … and some more coffee, please."

Claire took Marvin's cup and headed for the kitchen. Marvin picked up the remote control, turned on the television, and went through the stations until he came to a Red Sox game. It was the bottom of the seventh. Yankees were leading, 6-5. He glanced up at the clock again.

When Claire returned to the living room, she sat Marvin's plate and cup on the coffee table in front of him.

"You make the pie?" Marvin asked.

Claire sat on the couch. "No, it's from Lita's."

Marvin picked up the plate. "That Lita sure makes one helluva apple pie."

"She does," Claire agreed.

"My Mary, now she could make a pie," Marvin reminisced.

The two heard a vehicle pull up in front of the B&B, their heads turned toward the window.

"I wonder who that could be?" Claire said.

Marvin mumbled, "I dunno," over a mouthful of pie.

Claire got up and went to the window. "It's Ben!"

"Finally," Marvin mumbled, and shoved another bite of pie into his mouth.

"What do you men, finally?" Claire asked.

"What?"

"You said, 'finally.'"

"Finally *what*?" Marvin asked.

The front door opened, and Mica bolted down the stairs. "Ben, you're back!" he hollered.

"I'm back," Ben agreed.

Claire put her arms around Ben and kissed him. "We weren't expecting you back until tomorrow."

"I finished up early."

Mica reached for Ben's backpack. "Want me to take this?"

"No, I got it," Ben answered, pulling the pack closer to him. He stepped into the living room. "Any of that pie left?"

"Nope," Claire answered. "Our babysitter ate the last piece."

Ben played dumb. "Babysitter?"

Marvin shrugged. "I didn't say anything."

"What's going on?" Claire asked.

Marvin scooped up his last morsel of pie and shoved it into his homely kisser. "Well, I better get going."

"Thanks, Marv," Ben said, and patted him on the back as he walked by.

When the door shut, Claire reached over and turned the lock. "Mica, tell Ben goodnight, and you head on back up to bed."

"But Mom—"

"No butts, pal."

Mica hugged Ben and turned to climb the stairs. "Goodnight, Ben."

"Goodnight, Mica."

"I think we have a few things to discuss," Claire whispered to Ben.

"Like?"

"Like why you sent Marvin over here to sit with us until you got home, where you really were today, who was the girl I heard in the background making kissing noises,

147

and what's in that backpack that you didn't want Mica to see?"

"Wow," Ben said. "You don't miss much, do you?"

Chapter Thirty

That was our old friend Jimmy Buffett singing "A Pirate Looks at Forty," but you and I will be looking at a high of seventy-five today and mostly sunny. This is Big Larry Lincoln and you're listening to 104.2. We're the best morning radio program in Dunquin Cove because we're the only morning radio program in Dunquin Cove and todays show is brought to you by our good friends over at Petrelli and Pert. Feeling less than safe in an ever-changing world? Give the experts at Petrelli and Pert a call at 1-800-555-2321. With offices in Boston, Portland, and now Dunquin Cove, to handle your entire home and business security needs. Tell 'em Big Larry Lincoln sent ya.

Ben rolled over and smacked the snooze button. "I'll be sure to tell 'em, Larry." He pulled back the blankets, threw his legs over the edge of the bed, and slid his feet into his slippers. He glanced down at his small backpack that lay on the floor; he leaned over, stuffed it under the edge of the bed, and pulled the blankets down to conceal it.

"Good morning," Claire said when Ben walked into the kitchen.

"Morning. Why didn't you wake me up?"

"You looked exhausted last night, so I reset the alarm when I got up."

"Where is everyone?"

"Mr. Reagan was up and out the door by six. Mrs. Reagan had breakfast with Mica and me. She left at seven-thirty. And Mica is already out front with Marvin, working on the house."

Ben grinned. "You're a regular Dunquin Cove town crier, aren't you? He walked back into the dining room and poured himself a cup of coffee. "We're going to have to find some way to pay Marv back for all of his help on the house."

"There's a bag full of cash upstairs that says you might have found a way to pay him back."

Ben quickly looked around as though someone might overhear. "Shh!" he whispered. "Let's just keep the contents of that bag between you and me."

Claire laughed. "I know, I know. It was joke. Now, what can I make you for breakfast?"

"I'll just throw a couple Pop-Tarts in the toaster. I'm not that hungry, and I wanted to get over to Lenny's and talk to Artie about that painting job."

Claire opened the cupboard door above her and pulled out a box of s'mores flavored Pop-Tarts and held them out to Ben.

Ben turned up his nose. "Not those. Grab the ones with no frosting."

*****

Ben pulled his truck into the parking lot of Lenny's Garage and parked in front of one of the two overhead doors. Artie was in the garage with his head under the hood of an ancient Chevy Malibu rust bucket. He glanced around the side of the car and nodded to Ben; Ben waved back.

"Mornin', Artie," Ben said.

Artie wiped his hands on a red mechanic's rag that was sticking out of his back pocket. "Mornin', Ben. What brings you around this early? Nothing wrong with the truck, I hope."

"Nope. She runs like a top."

"Spins around and then falls over?" Artie joked.

"Good one. No, I got a call from Marvin last night telling me that you found something inside the flat."

Artie's eyes widened. "Oh yeah. Come in the office." Ben followed him in and Artie opened a drawer in his desk. "Look at this."

Ben took the sharp metal object from Artie and inspected it. "Found it in the tire, huh?"

"Yup, and it matches the puncture hole in the sidewall. Looks like someone stuck it in and the handle broke off when they tried to pull it out."

"Or maybe someone broke it off on purpose."

"What do you mean?"

"In prison shankings, it's common practice to break off the handle after you stab someone. That way, a guard or another inmate can't pull out the blade. Maybe the guy who did this was just acting out of habit."

"You're saying, maybe the guy who did this has been in prison before, and maybe he's even killed someone."

"Maybe."

"Ben … how come you know so much about stabbing someone in prison?"

Ben had to think quickly. "Picked it up binge-watching *Breaking Bad*."

Something caught Artie's attention over Ben's shoulder. Ben turned to look and saw two patrol cars drive by, light bars flashing.

"That's odd," Artie said.

"What's odd?" Ben asked.

"I've lived in this town my whole life and never saw two cop cars drive by at the same time with their lights on."

Together the two men walked out the front door. "They're stopping in front of the bakery," Ben observed.

Artie reached back around the door and flipped over a small cardboard clock that read, BE BACK SOON. "Come on," he said. "Let's go see what's going on."

Chapter Thirty-One

Ben burst through the door first. Chet was standing in the middle of the room, his eyes focused on the floor at a scattering of blood droplets. The rear entrance was standing open, and Ben could see Officer Ryan Marx standing in the alley.

"Chet, what's going on?" Ben asked.

Chet spun around and put up his hand. "Stop, Ben! This is a crime scene, for crying out loud."

Ben froze.

"A crime scene?" Artie asked. "What happened?"

"Where's Howard and Lita?" Ben asked.

"Are they okay?" Artie asked.

"Just slow down, guys, just slow down. Howard was attacked last night out behind the store. Someone beat him pretty bad."

"Yeah, someone," Ben said sarcastically.

"What's that supposed to mean?" Chet asked.

Ben pointed across the street to where a man in white coveralls was affixing letters to the window of a store front. The letters P-E-T-R, and, E had been applied in an arching pattern. "Don't you think it's a little strange that all these things start happening around the same time a security company sets up shop in town?" Ben observed.

"All what things?" Chet asked.

Artie jumped in. "Sign got broke over at the hardware store, window broken at the diner, and somebody stuck an ice pick in Ben's tire."

Chet looked confused. "An ice pick?"

"Howard said he saw someone snooping around out here the other night," Ben added.

"He didn't report anything," Chet said. "Did he say who it was?"

"He didn't get a good look at the guy; he said it was too dark."

"Maybe he should get those guys to install some motion sensor lighting out here for him," Marx hollered in.

Chet snickered.

"There's nothing to laugh at," said Ben gravely. They gave him a price, and then the very night he tells them he's not interested, he gets the shit kicked out of him in the alley."

"Don't ya think that's quite a coincidence, Chet?" Artie asked.

Chet shook his head. "Breaking a window and almost beating someone half to death is two completely different things, guys. Some kids probably vandalized that sign and window, and whoever did this to Howard is probably the guy he saw out here the other night. It doesn't sound like they're connected to me."

"You could at least question them, Chet," Artie said.

"Question them about what? I know, I'll walk over there and say, 'Hey, guys, welcome to town. Did you beat the hell out of Howard Tanner over at the bakery?'"

"Forget it, Chet," Ben said with a wave of his hand. "If you won't ask some questions, I will." He turned and headed for the door.

"Ben!" Chet yelled. "Don't do anything stupid!" Chet started to follow but Artie stopped him.

"Let him just ask a few questions, Chet," Artie said.

Chet pushed Artie aside. "Questions aren't what I'm afraid of."

Ben reached Petrelli and Pert's before Chet left the bakery. His jaw was clenched and rage pumped through his veins. He yanked the door open and went in. Petrelli sat at a desk at the back of the room, and Gannon was seated on a brown leather sofa against the left wall. Seated next to Gannon was a man Ben didn't know, and a fourth gentleman was sitting in a chair in front of Petrelli's desk, his back to Ben.

The two men Ben didn't recognize jumped to their feet and their hands went quickly inside their jackets. The man on the sofa was right-handed; the other man was a lefty. Gannon signaled his goons with a slight hand gesture and both pulled their hands from their coats.

Ben could tell by their facial expressions that they had been laughing when he barged in, which riled him even more. "Something funny?" he asked angrily.

"Why, Mr. Dunning," Gannon said. "Glad you could stop in. What can we do for you today?"

Ben took a step toward Gannon and the two unknown men moved closer together, forming a human road block that forced Ben to halt.

"Ben, this is Mr. Jones and Mr. Smith," Gannon said by way of introduction. "Mr. Jones, Mr. Smith, I would like to introduce you to Ben Dunning. Like us, he's a businessman here in town. He and his lovely wife Claire own The Colsome House Bed and Breakfast over on Shore Drive."

Ben felt no need to correct Gannon on him and Claire's relationship status. If he thought they were husband and wife, that was fine with him.

Ben moved closer to Gannon and Jones put a hand on Ben's shoulder. Ben grabbed Jones's hand with his left and in one swift move jabbed him in the throat with his middle and right index fingers, and then drove his right elbow into the side of Smith's head. Jones dropped to his knees, gasping for air, and Smith hit the floor, unconscious.

Just as Chet burst through the door, Ben gave Jones a shove and he fell over onto Smith.

"Hold it!" Chet shouted.

Ben froze and stared into Gannon's eyes. Gannon sat with his legs crossed, a devilish grin plastered across his face. Petrelli hadn't moved during the entire incident.

Gannon's mouth opened but Petrelli spoke first. "Officer Rose," he said. "How are you this morning?"

Ben's head turned toward Petrelli. It was the first time he had heard him speak. His voice was deep and authoritative.

Chet looked at the two men lying on the floor. "I'm fine, Mr. Petrelli. How is everything here?"

Jones climbed to his knees and shook Smith. "Hey," he said. Smith groaned and rolled onto his back.

"A slight misunderstanding," Petrelli explained. "But I think we've straightened it out."

"Do you or your associate want to press charges?" Chet asked.

"No, no, that won't be necessary, Officer. They're both fine."

"Yeah, Officer, it was just a misunderstanding," Jones said as he climbed to his feet. He reached out, grabbed Smith's hand, and pulled him up clumsily. The two goons shambled through a door at the back of the room.

Ben was still glaring at Petrelli. "Yeah, just a slight misunderstanding, Chet," he echoed, turned, and walked toward the door.

Artie was outside. He pulled the door open and held it as Ben walked out. "Feel better?" he asked.

"For now," Ben answered. "But this is far from over."

Chapter Thirty-Two

"Beautiful day to scrape a house," Marvin said, his sour expression suggesting anything but.

Ben swung the truck door shut.

"Yeah, Ben," Mica chimed in. "Beautiful day to scrape a house."

"Mica, run in the house and get your mother,' Ben said.

"Why?"

"Just do it." Ben's voice was stern, and Mica raced toward the front door.

Marvin sat his wire brush down on the top rung of the stepladder. "What's wrong, Ben?"

"Howard is in the hospital."

"Hospital? What happened?"

"Someone jumped him in the alley behind the store."

Marvin stepped down from the ladder. "How bad is it?"

"Chet said it was pretty bad but he should be okay. I'm going to head over there now and see if Lita needs anything."

"Good idea," Marvin agreed. "You mind if I tag along?"

"I don't want Claire and Mica here alone, Marv. I was wondering if you could stay with them."

"Sure, Ben, you go ahead."

When Mica returned with his mother, Ben explained the situation. On an impulse, he ran up the stairs into the house, skipping every other step.

Ben dropped to his knees at the edge of the bed, reached under, and pulled out the backpack. He unzipped it, reached inside, and pulled out the 9mm. Standing, he tucked the gun into the front of his waistband and adjusted his shirt over the weapon. He stepped back and glanced into the full-length floor mirror across the room, to make sure the gun wasn't noticeable. Satisfied, he left the room.

*****

Ben pushed the button for the fourth floor and the doors of the elevator slid shut. He hummed along with the Muzak version of "The Girl from Ipanema" drifting from the tinny-sounding speakers.

When the doors opened again Ben was staring down a long hallway. Gannon and Jones were stepping onto the elevator at the other end of the hall. Gannon turned, saw

Ben, smiled, and pointed his finger like a gun. He imitated the recoil as he pretended to shoot. Jones reached over, pushed the button, and the doors shut.

Ben instinctively felt for his pistol with one hand as he rapidly pushed the lobby button several times. The doors shut, and Ben watched the numbers above the door. Three … two … *Dammit*, Ben thought as the doors parted.

An orderly started to roll a gurney onto the elevator. Ben stepped aside. The orderly backed up, pulling the bed with him. "Tight squeeze," he said. "On second thought, I'd better take the next one. you go ahead, sir."

Ben pushed the lobby button again. When the doors opened, Gannon and Jones were nowhere in sight. He ran to the lobby window overlooking the parking lot. *Shit!*

When Ben returned to the fourth floor, he went directly to the nurse's station. "Can you tell me what room Howard Tanner is in, please?"

A nurse, whom Ben was obviously bothering, sighed and removed her glasses. "Who?" she asked.

"Tanner, Howard Tanner."

"Are you family?"

"Do I have to be?"

"No."

"Then why did you ask?"

The woman shrugged her shoulders. "He's in Room 406"—she pointed lackadaisically—"that way."

"Thanks. I'll be sure to nominate you for nurse of the month."

Howard lay in his hospital bed. Tubes led to his nostrils and wires ran under his gown. A plastic clip on his index finger measured his pulse and oxygen saturation. An IV bag hanging from a pole ran to the back of his hand. His eyes were closed. Lita sat in a chair at his bedside, her face pale and careworn.

"Lita," Ben said softly.

She looked up from the pocketbook that was sitting on her lap. "Ben. Thanks for coming."

"How's he doing?"

Lita sighed like someone with the weight of the world on her shoulders. "He's in and out. He'll open his eyes and look around and then close them again. That's about it."

"What are the doctors saying?"

"He has three broken ribs and his left lung was collapsed. Took a nasty blow to the head. His nose is broken, too. The doctor said it looked like someone kicked him in the face a few times."

Ben walked over to the edge of the bed and placed his hand on top of Howard's. "Chet said the doctor says he should make a full recovery," he remarked.

Lita nodded and smiled at her husband. "Thank God, he inherited that hard German head from his mother."

Ben smiled. "Who found him, Lita?"

"I did. He never came home last night, so around nine, I called. He didn't answer the phone, so I walked over. The front door of the bakery was unlocked, and when I went in I saw the back door to the alley was standing open. He was just lying there." Lita burst into tears. "I thought he was dead, Ben. Who would do this? Why?"

Ben removed his hand from Howard's and walked over to Lita's side and knelt down. "Lita," he asked quietly. "Did two men stop here to see Howard just before I arrived?"

Lita cocked her head. "Yes. Why?"

"What did they want?"

"Well, one of them waited in the hall. The other man was the one who gave Howard the estimate for the security system. He said he just wanted to stop by to see how Howard was doing, Gannon, I think his name is. He said if there was anything we needed to just let him know."

Ben looked back over his shoulder at Howard. "I'll find the person responsible for this, Lita. I promise."

Lita took Ben's hand and squeezed. "When you do," she said, her voice breaking, "you make them pay."

Chapter Thirty-Three

It was a little after two when Ben walked into the Dunquin Cove Police Department. The squad room was empty. He stood with his palms on the counter, wishing there was a bell to ring for service. "Hello?" he called out.

At the back, past the four desks that furnished the squad room, was a door that read CHIEF OF POLICE. Ben rounded the counter and made his way through the desks and to the door. He opened it and went in. Chet was sitting at a desk, talking on the phone; he didn't look happy.

Ben waited at the door, hoping it was going to be a quick call.

"I gotta go," Chet said, and hung up the phone. "Can't you knock, Dunning?"

"Where is everybody?" Ben asked, looking back into the squad room.

Chet leaned back in his chair. "Everybody?" he repeated. "Who is everybody?"

"Well… is there an investigator working on Howard's case?"

Chet threw his head back and laughed. "Investigator? There's no investigator. For Chrissakes, since Buck retired we don't even have a police chief. Why do you think I'm sitting here? Interim Police Chief, that's what the selectmen call me."

"So, who's handling the case?"

"You're looking at him."

Ben pondered the situation. "How many cops does this town have?"

"With Buck gone and Lester out on sick leave, we only got me, Marx, Devlin, and Stella working dispatch."

"Why don't they hire a dispatcher and put Stella on patrol?"

"Why don't you go to a town meeting and ask?"

"Touché'. Is there anything I can do?"

"Afraid not, Ben," Chet answered. "If I asked for your help and then something happened to you, or to somebody else, I could lose my job and the town could get sued."

"Then you better not ask," Ben concluded.

"Right."

"So where are you on Howard's beating?"

"Well, Lita left the bakery around six and walked home, like she does almost every night. Howard stayed and closed up, like he does almost every night. When he took the garbage out to the dumpster, someone hit him in the head with something. Lita returned to the bakery about nine-thirty and found him lying there."

"If this happened last night then why didn't you show up until this morning?"

"I got an anonymous call last night; probably just before Howard was attacked."

"Anonymous call?"

"Yeah. The caller said they saw someone suspicious walking along the road about four miles out of town on Winding Hill Road. I was the only one here so I took a ride out there."

"Obviously someone just trying to get you out of town."

"Obviously. Then I was at the hospital most of the night. When I finally got a hold of Marx, I had him run over to the bakery and lock it up till I could get there."

Ben shook his head. "What did they hit Howard with?"

"Don't know."

"Anybody see anything?"

"Don't know that either. Marx is out now talking with anyone who might have been in the area at that time. But even if someone was walking by, they probably wouldn't have seen anything or anyone in the alley. It's dark as hell back there."

"Lita said she has been trying to get Howard to put a light out there for years."

Chet raised an eyebrow. "Someone was *going* to install some lights out there for him, but *somebody* talked him out of it."

"Hey, you can't blame this on me."

"All I know is that if you hadn't stuck your nose into Howard's business, he might not be lying in a hospital bed right now."

The glass double doors swung open. Chet looked past Ben and Ben turned.

"Back from lunch, Chief!" Stella called out. Stella Raines stood exactly five foot short and was about the same width. Ben glanced down at her gun belt and wondered if it was special order. Her long red hair was pulled back into a tight ponytail that stopped at the third roll of her back fat. She was in her late fifties and had been employed by the Dunquin Cove Police department since her father became the Chief of Police thirty-five years ago, and she had never drawn her gun in the line of duty.

"Don't call me Chief!" Chet hollered back.

"Sorry, Chief. It won't happen again." Stella gave Ben a wink as she pulled off her sweater, which could double as a tent, and hung it on the coat rack next to the front door. "Any calls while I was at lunch?"

Chet glanced over at his notes. "The Marchs' cat is still missing, Earl Foster is still hearing voices in his phone, and Mrs. Brill keeps throwing her dog's shit into the street."

Stella sat at her desk. "Those voices are in Earl's head, not in his phone."

Ben stepped back out of Chet's office. "Well, I can see that you two have your hands full here with cats, dogs, and voices, so I'm going to head back over to the hospital and speak with the doctor that was on call last night when they brought Howard in. Do you think you could give them a ring and let them know I'm coming?"

"I can do that, Ben, but don't do anything that's gonna make me look stupid."

"You don't need his help for that," Stella chimed in.

"You know what I mean. I don't want anything blowing back on me. If you insist on playing cop, you're doing so in an unofficial capacity."

"You have nothing to worry about, Chief," Ben replied over his shoulder on his way out.

Chapter Thirty-Four

Ben stood in the alley behind the bakery, staring up at the sides of the buildings. The only alley in town, it ran from Shore Drive to Dunquin Lane behind the bakery, a candy store, a wine shop that sold wines from local vineyards, and The Cove restaurant. On the opposite side of the alley was a six-foot stockade fence, and beyond that fence were the back yards of the homes on Flagg Street.

Ben crouched down and looked under each dumpster, and then inside each one, as he made his way toward Dunquin Lane. He scanned the ground as he walked along.

When he came to the end he turned left onto Dunquin, walked the half block to Main Street, and made another left. When he arrived at the front of the bakery he tried the door; it was locked. The sign hanging in the window still said OPEN. Ben wondered how many people would try to enter today, not knowing what had happened to Howard.

"How's he doin'?" someone called out.

Ben turned to see John Morgan standing in front of the market, his big, meaty fingers wrapped around a cigar. As usual, John's cheeks were red enough to guide any sleigh through a foggy night. High blood pressure, Ben figured. John's white apron was stained red with the blood of some dead cow or pig.

"He'll live," Ben called back.

John pressed his thumb against the side of his nose and blew out a snot rocket. Ben could hear the smack as it hit the sidewalk. *Appetizing*, Ben thought. *Two steaks, please.*

"Hard German head," John said.

Ben glanced toward Petrelli and Pert's storefront as he stepped off of the curb and started across the street. He could see Gannon standing in the front window, his arms folded in front of him. He was staring at Ben. Ben felt a slight sense of accomplishment. If they weren't worried, they wouldn't be watching.

Ben put out his hand and John Morgan did the same.

"Smoke break?" Ben asked.

"Yup," John answered.

"Were you out here last night?"

"You mean around the time Howard got his brains bashed in?"

Ben winced. "Yeah, that's what I meant."

"Chet already asked. The store stays open till nine on Fridays. I walked out here once about seven-thirty. The lights were on in the bakery, and I could see Howard through the window, mopping the floor. I locked up about quarter after nine and drove home. I passed Lita walking on Shore Drive. I waved, and she waved back."

169

"She was on her way to see why Howard wasn't home yet."

John took a long drag on the stogie. "Curt and Artie think it's got something to do with these new guys down the street," he said, pointing toward Petrelli and Pert's office."

"Me too," Ben agreed.

"What are we gonna do about it?"

"We?"

"Yeah, *we*." John said. "Maybe it's about time we show these gentlemen they're fuckin' with the wrong town."

John's arms were like corded steel, a benefit of wrestling animal carcasses and cutting them up into little pieces all of his life. Ben wouldn't want to tangle with him. "We need proof," he said.

John flicked his cigar into the gutter and stared into Ben's eyes. "There's two ways to acquire proof: Wait for it to happen, or cause it to happen."

"Who said that?" Ben asked.

"Me," John answered.

Chapter Thirty-Five

When Ben pulled into the driveway of the B&B, Marvin and Mica had already finished for the day and the ladders were leaning against the foundation of the house. The sun had gone down but darkness hadn't set in yet. Ben inspected their work as he made his way to the front door; they were making good progress. When he entered, he went directly to the bedroom to put away the 9mm and then searched the house for Claire. He found her in the backyard, drinking a beer with Marvin. Mica sat at the picnic table, his face in his tablet, playing a game.

"What's going on back here?" Ben asked.

Claire turned her head and held up her beer bottle. "Want a brew?"

"Sounds good."

"Good," Marvin said. "Grab us another one too."

Claire chuckled.

Ben turned back toward the house. "Coming right up."

"Bring out some chips or something," Marvin called after him.

Ben scratched the back of his head with his middle finger.

"I saw that!" Marvin hollered.

When Ben returned to the group he handed them their beers, tossed the Doritos in Marvin's lap, and sat at the table across from Mica, who never lifted his head from the tablet.

"How's Howard doing?" Claire asked.

"He was still unconscious when I was there, but the doctors are saying he will make a full recovery."

Marvin stuffed a handful of chips into his mouth and chomped noisily. "That hard German head," he mumbled.

"So I've heard," Ben concurred.

Marvin asked, "How's Lita holding up?"

"Good as can be expected. She's going to stay at the hospital tonight."

"What are the police saying?"

"They're saying that they're short-staffed."

Marvin snickered. "I bet Chet is wishing old Buck was still behind the desk."

"He does seem a little overwhelmed," Ben agreed.

Marvin took a swig of his beer. "Maybe it's time we offered him a little help."

"I offered."

"Did he accept?"

"Not officially."

"I'll take that as a yes."

Just then, sirens sounded off in the distance.

"What now?" Claire asked.

"Sounds like fire trucks," Marvin remarked.

"Look!" Mica said, pointing over Marvin's house at the orange glow in the sky.

"Where is that?" Ben asked.

"Farmwell's?" Claire suggested.

"Maybe the diner," Marvin said.

Ben stood just as a fireball shot into the sky; a second later they heard the explosion. "Lenny's Garage!" Ben said. "Come on, Marv."

The two men sprinted to Ben's truck and headed in the direction of the fire.

*****

It *was* Lenny's Garage, and Ben could get no closer to the fire than the corner of Shore Drive and Main Street. He pulled to the curb, and he and Marvin walked closer. Officers Marx and Devlin were doing their best to keep back the crowd that was beginning to form. Chet was across the street in front of Farmwell's, talking with Artie. Ben made his way through the crowd toward the two men.

Another, smaller explosion erupted, shattering the front windows and the entire group of onlookers flinched.

"Is there anything I can do?" Ben asked.

"Just stay back," Chet ordered.

Ben could feel the warmth of the fire on his face, carried by the breeze, the mist from the fire hoses fell like a light spring rain over the crowd. Many people held their shirts up over their noses to escape the sickening stink of the burning tires inside the garage.

"What happened?" Marvin asked.

Curt Holliday ran by, dressed in his fire gear, as he directed others where to point their hoses.

"I don't know," Artie shouted over the commotion. "I walked down to The Cove to get something to eat for dinner. I was on my way back here to get my car when I saw the flames and smoke. By the time the fire department got here, it was fully engulfed." He turned to watch the fire and then hung his head down. "Lenny is gonna be so pissed."

"He'll just be glad no one was hurt," Marvin said, and patted Artie on the back.

Ben scanned the crowd. Standing in the street at the intersection of Main and Shore was Gannon. He pulled a cigar from his inside coat pocket, bit off the tip, and spit it into the street. He searched his pocket and pulled out a pack of matches. His eyes met Ben's. He lit the cigar, held up the lit match, and, grinning, blew it out. He turned and walked back toward his own business.

John Morgan walked up behind Marvin and Ben. His heavy fire coat was unbuttoned. He removed his fire helmet and wiped the sweat from his sooty brow with his coat sleeve. "We're getting it under control," he informed

Chet, and then looked at Ben. "Wait for it to happen, or cause it to happen." Morgan put his hat back on, turned, and walked back toward the fire.

"John!" Ben called out.

John stopped in the middle of the street and looked back.

"Swing by the B&B tomorrow morning around eight—we'll talk about it."

John nodded and continued on his way

"What was that about?" Chet asked.

"Nothing for you to worry about, Chief," Ben answered.

A waitress pushed open the door of the White Rose Diner and shoved a shim under it to hold it open. She went back inside and when she reappeared, she was carrying a tray filled with coffee in to-go cups. She walked up to Chet and asked, "Officer Rose, would you like a cup of coffee?"

Chet took a cup. "Thanks, Tammy."

Tammy smiled and continued through the crowd, handing out the free coffee and making sure any firefighter that wanted one got theirs first.

Ben watched as the town pulled together to help one of their own.

"You should think about joining," Marvin said.

"What, the fire department?" Ben asked.

"Sure. Why not? They could always use the help."

"I'm surprised you're not out there."

"I was the Fire Chief for eight years," Marvin reminisced. "But it's a young man's game, Ben. It's young, strong men like you, John, and Curt that keep a town safe."

Ben smirked. "I do believe that's the first compliment you've ever paid me, Marv.

"Hmph! I didn't mean for it to come out that way."

Chapter Thirty-Six

Claire was setting the chafing dishes on the buffet for breakfast when she heard the knock on the front door. The front door opened and she looked into the hall. It was John Morgan.

"In here, John!" Claire called out.

The floor creaked beneath John's feet as he strode down the hall.

"Ben around?" John asked, poking his head into the dining room.

"He just ran upstairs; he should be down any minute. Can I get you a cup of coffee?"

"Sure, that would be great."

"Sit down," Claire said, and went back into the kitchen. When she returned, she sat the steaming mug of coffee in front of John.

"Thanks, Claire."

"There's cream and sugar on the buffet. Help yourself."

"I drink it black."

Ben walked down the stairs and into the dining room. "Come on, John, Marvin is waiting for us at his house."

John picked up his mug, thanked Claire once again, and the two men headed out the front door.

Ben was first up the steps at Marvin's house. John looked back at the familiar car parked in the street. "Curt Holliday is here too?" he asked.

Ben pounded on the door. "Yeah, and Artie was going to be here but he had to meet with Lenny this morning about the garage."

"Come in!" Marvin hollered. "It's unlocked for Chrissakes."

"Wait for me!" Alan Cobb yelled from across the street.

John rolled his eyes. "Who invited him?"

Ben opened the front door. "Must have been Marv. They're thick as thieves, even if they do get on each other's nerves."

"That Cobb is one annoying son of a bitch," John noted.

"Hey, Ben. Hey John," Cobb said.

"Hey, Cobb," Ben and John said in unison and the three men went inside.

Cobb pulled out the chair at the head of the table.

Marvin cleared his throat. "That's my chair."

"Sorry," Cobb said and took another seat.

All five men sat around the table, with Marvin at the head, Cobb to his right, and Ben to his left. John Morgan sat next to Ben, and Curt Holliday sat at foot of the table.

"Who wants to go first?" Curt asked.

John spoke up. "I think we can all agree that Petrelli and his goons have to go."

All of the men nodded in agreement.

"I think we should let the police handle this," Cobb said.

John rolled his eyes and looked at Ben. "See what I mean?"

"What's that supposed to mean?" Cobb shot back.

"It means if you're not here to help, then go home," John answered, his eyes like flints.

"The cops can't help, Cobb," Marvin explained. "They need the evidence; we don't. Should we just sit around and do nothing until these guys mess up and the cops *can* do something? What if they don't screw up? Whose business burns next? Who gets jumped in an alley next?"

John slammed his hand on the table. "This stops now!"

Cobb shook his head emphatically. "Okay, okay, I'm in, but what do we do?"

The men all looked to Ben. "We *cause* them to screw up," he said with a wink in John's direction.

"How do we do that?" Curt asked.

"I have a plan," Ben said.

Chapter Thirty-Seven

It was Monday morning, a few minutes after nine, when Ben Dunning walked into the Dunquin Cove office of Petrelli and Pert.

"Good morning, Mr. Dunning. Do you have an appointment?" Gannon asked with the usual shit-eating grin. Just like the last time Ben barged in, he was sitting in the same spot on the leather sofa against the adjacent wall. Petrelli was at his desk, pen in hand, jotting something down in a leather binder.

Ben scanned the room quickly. There was no sign of Tweedledee and Tweedledumb, or as Gannon referred to them, Smith and Jones. "No," he answered. "I didn't think I would need one. After all, you don't seem to be very busy."

"Don't worry, Ben. May I call you Ben?" Gannon asked. He didn't wait for an answer. "Business will pick up soon enough. It always does. At first people think, this is a safe place to live—we have no need for security systems, cameras, alarms, and such. But then, sooner or later,--usually sooner—dumb hicks like these—" Gannon made a sweeping gesture to indicate the whole town— "pull their heads out of their asses and take a look around. They see a broken window, or perhaps they see a close friend get beaten. God only knows who. Maybe a friend's business, a place where he's worked his whole life, gets burned to the ground."

Ben showed no emotion. "That's why I'm here, gentlemen, to tell you that it all ends today. You close up shop, you take your goons, and you get out of town."

Petrelli laid his pen down on the desk, shut the binder, and zipped it closed. He leaned back in his chair and put his feet on the desk. "Dunning," he began, breaking from character and speaking in a thick "Joisey" accent. "Let me tell you a story about a little town a few miles from the Jersey shore. We opened an office there about three years ago. It was a small town, around eleven thousand people, a town just like this one. At first *they* didn't think they needed our help either. Within a couple of weeks, a few random events helped change their minds.

"We got a client here, a client there, but we weren't doing the business we thought we should be doing. Come to find out, there was this guy in town, like you, who was going around bad-mouthing us. He was yapping to anyone who would listen that they shouldn't trust us, that *we* caused the increase in crime. What was his name, Gannon?"

"Mark Snyder," Gannon answered. "A real American hero."

"All towns aren't the same, Petrelli," Ben said.

Petrelli held up his finger. "You see, Dunning, that's where you're wrong. All of these shitty little towns are just alike."

181

"All alike," Gannon repeated.

"Can you get on with the story?" Ben asked. "I want to get going so you two can pack up."

Petrelli stood and leaned forward, his palms on the desk, gaudy pinky rings decorating either hand. "The gentleman I was telling you about, the big mouth like you, he was beat to death one night, right on Main Street, when two men tried to rob him."

Ben glared unblinkingly into Petrelli's eyes. "I bet business really picked up after that."

"The assholes eventually gave us a plaque for making their town safer," Gannon laughed. "Can you believe it? A goddamn plaque."

"So what I'm trying to say here, Dunning," Petrelli continued, "is that you're going to help us one way or another. You can help by keeping your mouth shut, or you can help in the same way that Mr. Snyder did."

Ben smiled. "Like I said, gentlemen, be out of town by the end of today." He turned and walked out the door.

On his way out he feinted a jab at Gannon. The big man flinched, and, to cover embarrassment, fussed with his tie.

"That motherfucker is mine, Boss," he said when Ben was gone.

"All in good time, Marco, all in good time."

*****

A little after noon, John Morgan was cutting a prime rib into Delmonico steaks. He paused, looked up at the clock above the bandsaw, and then stabbed the knife into the butcher block. He walked over to the phone and dialed.

A recorded female voice said. "Thank you for calling Petrelli and Pert. To reach our Boston office, please press one. For our Portland office, please press two, and for our Dunquin Cove office, please press three."

John pressed three.

"Petrelli and Pert, how can I help you?"

"This is John Morgan. I own the Village Market on Main Street."

"Yes, Mr. Morgan. This is Marco Gannon. What can we do for you today?"

"I just wanted to let you gentlemen know that I've looked over the estimate you gave me, and I've decided to go with someone else."

"Someone else? Who?"

"Ben Dunning. His estimate was a little cheaper, and he's local, so I've decided to go with him. Thanks for your time." John hung up the phone and turned to Ben, who was leaning against the wall, his arms folded across his chest. "How was that?"

"Perfect," Ben answered.

*****

At nine o'clock that same night, Sam O'Brien picked up the phone that sat at the end of the bar. When the call connected he listened to the instructions and pressed three.

"Petrelli and Pert, how can I help you?"

"This is Sam O'Brien over at The Cove," he said in a disgusted tone. "I heard something out in the alley behind the restaurant, and when I went to look at the monitor there was just static—no picture. It looks like the light isn't working either."

"Did you go out and have a look?" Gannon asked.

Sam snorted. "I'm not going out there after what happened to Howard Tanner."

"Well, what would you like us to do, Mr. O'Brien? If you heard something in the alley, call the police."

"I'm calling *you*. *You* put in the cameras, now get *your* ass over here and see what's going on, or I'll call the bank and cancel the check I gave you."

"I'll send my guys over to have a look," Gannon said. *Click!*

"Perfect," Ben said, and downed the last of his beer. "Let's take our places, men."

Chapter Thirty-Eight

Smith and Jones walked through the front door of The Cove restaurant. They didn't look too happy about a maintenance call at nine o'clock on a Sunday night.

"What's the problem?" Jones asked.

Sam jerked a thumb over his shoulder. "There was someone snooping around out there in back. Fat lot of good that shit you guys sold me did—nothing's working. I should stop payment on that check."

"I wouldn't do that if I was you," Jones said.

"Mr. Gannon would not be too happy," Smith added as he and Jones walked past Sam and through the kitchen.

Sam followed them to the back door and when they walked out, he closed the door behind them and locked it.

Smith quickly spun around and tried the doorknob. "O'Brien!" he called out.

"Good evening, gentlemen," Ben said. They both turned to see him step out from behind the dumpster. They went for their guns. "Don't even think about it," Ben warned, as he raised his weapon.

"What is this?" Smith demanded.

"Are you really that stupid?" Ben replied, and then whistled.

Curt Holliday and Alan Cobb walked into the alley from Dunquin Lane, Curt held a baseball bat in his right hand and repeatedly smacked it into his left as the two men walked toward Ben.

"Mr. Gannon will kill you," Jones said.

"Lace your fingers behind your heads," Ben ordered.

Smith did as he was told. Jones didn't move.

Curt swung his bat into the back of Jones's legs. He buckled and dropped to his knees.

"Do what he tells you or the next one will be upside your head," Curt said.

Jones, moaning in agony, quickly laced his hands behind his head.

"Good boy," Cobb said.

"Reach into their jackets," Ben told Cobb, "and take out their weapons." He glanced over at Curt. "If either one of them moves put it out of the park."

"You know it," Curt answered.

Cobb removed their pistols and stepped back.

Ben waved his gun toward the rear entrance of the bakery. "Come on."

When they got to the back door, Ben knocked. The door opened and John Morgan said, "Come on in, boys, your seats are ready."

Smith and Jones entered first, followed by Ben and the others. John led them to two chairs that sat back to back in the kitchen, where Marvin was waiting. The entire bakery was dark except for a dimly lit sconce on the wall over the sink.

"Have a seat, boys," Marvin said.

"What's going on?" Jones asked. "You won't get away with this."

Curt raised his bat. "He said, 'Have a seat.'"

They sat.

"John, Marvin," said Ben, "tie their hands behind their backs and their ankles to the chair legs."

John bound Smith while Marvin did the same to Jones.

Ben patted them down searching for their cell phones. Smith's was in his shirt pocket, and Jones kept his in his pants pocket. Ben fumbled through the settings, pushing different icons. "Does anyone know how to record on one of these things?" he finally asked.

Curt set his bat down and took the phones and tapped each screen a few times. "Touch the little picture of a microphone when you're ready to record," he said and handed them back to Ben.

Ben looked at Smith. "When I start recording, I'm going to ask you a series of questions. If I don't like the answer you give, I will give Mr. Holliday a nod and he will hit Mr. Jones very hard with his bat. Do you understand?"

Smith didn't answer.

Curt grabbed his bat.

"That was question number one," Ben informed him, and nodded to Curt.

He slammed the bat into Jones' shin; the goon screamed in pain.

"God damn you!" Smith shouted.

"Maybe you had better put a gag in Jones's mouth," Ben suggested. "He might be doing a lot of screaming tonight."

Marvin grabbed a rag from a drawer and stuffed it in Jones's mouth.

"Let's try again," Ben said. "Do you understand?"

Smith nodded yes.

Ben looked at the phone. "The screen went dark," he said.

"Give me that," Curt said, laying down the bat and yanking the phone from Ben's hand. "Press the button on the side and the screen lights up, then press the microphone." He handed the phone back to Ben. "Sheesh, Ben, it's the twenty-first century. Get with the program!"

"Sorry," Ben said. "I just have one of those flip phones." Ben tapped the microphone and then did the same thing on Jones's phone, so that both cells were recording.

Curt picked up his bat again.

Ben placed both phones in Smith's shirt pocket. "What's you real name?"

"Smith."

Ben nodded.

Curt aimed for Jones's other shin and swung. The goon let out a muffled scream and stared pitifully at his partner with wild, desperate eyes.

"Sutherland!" Smith shouted. "Rory Sutherland."

"And what is your friend's name?"

"Leland Sutherland."

Ben smiled. "No wonder you're so protective. Younger brother?"

Smith shook his head yes.

"Who beat Howard Tanner?"

"We both did."

"Who told you to do it?"

Smith didn't answer.

Ben nodded. Curt adopted a home run stance.

"Gannon!" Smith shouted. "Marco Gannon!"

It was a split second too late, and Curt brought the bat down on Jones's lap.

The goon groaned and bit down fiercely on the rag. Tears poured out of his tightly shut eyes.

"We beat up Tanner, we broke the sign, we smashed the window, and we burned down the gas station!" Smith yelled. "We did it all! Just stop hitting him, for Chrissakes!"

"And Gannon hired you to do it all?"

"Yes."

"Who else?"

"Mr. Petrelli. He and Gannon hire us to commit crimes so that they can sell their security shit. We install the cameras, monitors, and lighting and stuff. Everyone signs a one year agreement and sends them a fee every month. When the year is almost up we move on to another town."

"How long have you been doing this?"

"Gannon and Petrelli have been doing it for about eight years. We've been their muscle the whole time."

"How many towns?"

"This is the sixth or seventh."

"Spill the names. Quick!"

After jogging his memory, Smith stuttered out the list.

"And you've never had the feds after you?"

"We've felt the heat, sure. But Gannon and Petrelli have Mob connections. They always manage to beat the rap through legal loopholes and technicalities and shit like that." he paused and added smugly, "They're smart guys— smarter than any of you. If you amateurs think you're gonna take them down, think again."

Curt brandished his bat. "Want me to smack him, Ben?"

"No, a man is entitled to his fantasies," said Ben. He picked up the cell phones and ended the recording.

"I've given you what you wanted," said Smith. "Are you going to let us go?"

Ben placed the cell phones in his pocket. "Not just yet. Now you have to answer to the rest of these men for putting one of their good friends in the hospital."

"I don't." Sam grabbed his jacket that hung on the inside of the kitchen door and put it on. "Cards tomorrow night?"

"You can bet on it," Ben answered.

Sam zipped up his jacket and, brushing his index finger across his temple and pointing it at Ben, walked out the front door.

Ben glanced down at the floor beneath him and the wall behind him. He stood, turned around, and bent over. With his knuckles, he rapped on the wall a few times and then tapped the wall with the toe of his shoe, just above the base board. "Hmm," he said quietly. "I wonder how thick this wall is."

*****

An hour had gone by. Both of the cell phones had rung twice, and Ben even had to refill his glass.

Ben felt the cool spring night air as Marco Gannon pushed open the door to The Cove restaurant. Gannon, wearing his long black overcoat, stepped inside and looked around the room. He saw Ben sitting at the end of the bar and made his way across the dining room to the kitchen door, always keeping Ben in view. He pushed open the kitchen door, glanced inside, and then let the door swing shut.

"Looking for someone?" Ben asked.

Gannon leaned against the bar. "No bartender?"

"He left early. Help yourself."

Gannon went behind the bar, poured himself a bourbon, neat, in a rocks glass, and then returned to the other side of the bar.

Ben picked up one of the cell phones, tapped play, and slid it down the bar. Gannon could hear Smith's voice before the phone came to rest a foot in front of him.

As the recording played, Gannon downed his drink and then slammed his empty glass on the phone, smashing it to pieces.

"Now why did you go and do that?" said Ben. He held up the other phone. "Luckily I've got a spare. And it's got the same program on it. All about two dickheads from Joisey and their racketeering schemes. How they take advantage of decent people in small towns to line their filthy pockets. A real thriller—tonight's the finale."

"What is wrong with you?" Gannon asked.

"I must be crazy," Ben answered.

Gannon smiled. "You must be. Why would anyone think this shithole of a town is worth dying for?"

Ben pressed play on the other phone. "That's what *I* was wondering about *you*."

When Gannon heard Smith's voice on the other phone, the smile left his face and rage filled his eyes. Gannon yanked his pistol from his shoulder holster faster than Ben had expected.

Ben dove to the floor, grabbing his gun, as Gannon fired, exploding the beer glass.

Gannon fired a second time and then continued to fire as he walked the length of the bar. As he came around the end, he pointed the gun at the floor. Ben was gone. Gannon's eyes widened when he saw the hole Ben had kicked in the wall; just large enough for a man to crawl through.

Gannon stepped back and turned. Ben was standing in the hallway that led to the bathrooms.

As Gannon raised his weapon, Ben fired four times into his chest, sending him stumbling backwards. He tottered for a few moments like a stubborn ten pin and crashed to the floor on his back, setting of a chorus of jangling glasses behind the bar.

"The bigger they are," said Ben, "the more noise the lousy bastards make when they fall."

Chapter Forty

Three patrol cars, lights flashing, sat on Main Street. One car was in front of Lita's Bakery, and the other two were parked in the middle of the street in front of the Petrelli and Pert storefront. An ambulance was parked in front of The Cove.

Officer Marx put his hand on the top of Petrelli's head and guided him into the back seat of his patrol car.

Officer's Chet Rose and Stella Raines escorted Smith and Jones from the bakery. Jones could hardly walk, and both men had been beaten heavily. "Looks like these two put up one hell of a fight," Chet remarked.

"It was quite a brawl," Marvin agreed.

"And yet none of you have a mark on you," Chet added.

"Are you kidding?" Marvin said, holding out his hands. "Look at my poor knuckles!"

"And you should see my poor bat," Curt whispered to John Morgan. John laughed.

After Smith and Jones were in the car, Ben handed the cell phone to Chet. "It's all on here," he said.

Ben and the others stood in the street and watched as the three patrol cars sped back toward the police station.

"C'mon Marv, we better get home. We gotta get up early tomorrow and paint a house," Ben said.

Marvin slapped Ben on the back. "Right behind ya, pal."

Curt turned to John. "Come on, John, I'll give you a ride home." He and John started up the street toward Curt's car

"Can I get a ride, Curt?" Cobb asked.

"No," Curt answered.

"Come on."

"Nope, we're not going that way. Walk with them," Curt said, pointing at Ben and Marvin.

"I don't want to listen to him bitch all the way home," Marvin hollered over his shoulder.

"But Marv, we're drinking buddies!" Cobb protested.

"But you can be a royal pain in the ass," said Marvin. He turned to Ben. "Right, pal?"

"Leave me out of this."

"You guys are all assholes!" Cobb yelled as Ben and Marvin took off running.

Chapter Forty-One

Ben walked out onto the front porch Tuesday morning and picked up the newspaper. As he turned and made his way down the hall to the dining room he flipped through the pages, scanning the headlines. When he got to the fourth page he paused and read the headline: DORCHESTER MOTHER AND DAUGHTER MURDERED IN THEIR HOME.

God dammit.

He stood in the hall next to the phone stand, reading the story. The police thought it was a burglary gone bad. There was no mention of the four men Ben had killed. He wondered why.

The phone rang and Ben continued to read.

On the second ring, Claire hollered from the kitchen. "Ben, can you get that?"

Ben closed the paper. "Colsome House Bed and Breakfast."

"Ben?"

"Yes. Who's this?"

"Bob Phillips."

"Hey, Bob, what's going on? Enjoying your retirement?"

"Can't complain. Ben, I was talking with a buddy of mine from Boston. He was telling me that someone murdered the son of an Irish mobster three days ago. The Mick is turning the city upside down trying to find the guy who killed him. He's making a lot of noise and even put a bounty on the guy's head. A few witnesses gave a description of the guy and the truck he was driving."

"They did, did they?"

"Yeah, they did. The description sounded a lot like you, Ben."

"Huh, what a coincidence."

"Just thought I would give you a heads up."

"Thanks, Bob."

"Take care of yourself, Ben. If you need anything, just call."

"I will. Bye, Bob."

"Bye."

Ben placed the receiver back in the cradle.

Claire walked out into the dining room. "Who was that?"

"Wrong number."

The End

COMING DECEMBER 2015

Double Trouble

From the Tales of Dan Coast

COMING SPRING 2016

Jake Stellar

When Death Returns

ALSO BY RODNEY RIESEL

Sleeping Dogs Lie

From the Tales of Dan Coast

A mystery set in the Florida Keys follows Dan Coast, an unlicensed private detective of sorts, as he is hired to find the missing boyfriend of a woman who herself soon ends up missing. When someone from the woman's past unexpectedly shows up at Dan's home, with a story of faked deaths and missing life insurance money; Dan along with his sidekick Red set out to find the money, and the woman.

ISBN: 978-0-9883503-0-4

Ocean Floors

From the Tales of Dan Coast

The second installment in the Dan Coast series, Ocean Floors, is a tale of mystery and possible romance when a chance meeting with a beautiful young woman leads Dan and his trusted sidekick Red down a road of murder and kidnapping. Join Dan and Red as they try to solve the murder while searching for a missing friend.

ISBN: 978-0-9894877-0-2

Impaled

An Adirondack Short Story

Eric Stone is an investigator with The Town of Webb Police Department. Chuck Little is Head Ranger at the Nick's Lake campground. An unlikely duo, together they work to solve a murder that mimics a spree of gruesome murders taking place years earlier. Is it a copycat, or has the murderer resurfaced after all of these years? Join Stone and Little as they piece together the clues to solve this mystery taking place in the small village of Old Forge in the Adirondack Mountains.

North Murder Beach

A Jake Stellar Novel

The first installment of the story of North Myrtle Beach police detective, Jake Stellar. The spring bike rallies have ended, the spring breakers have all gone back to school, and the summer tourist season is a few weeks away. What better time for a police officer to take a nice quiet relaxing week off from work? That's what Jake Stellar had in mind. That is until someone from his past resurfaces to remind him of a terrible secret he has spent years trying to forget. In North Murder Beach, a story of revenge, Jake is unwillingly and violently forced to confront his secret from his past.

ISBN: 978-0-9894877-1-9

The Coast of Christmas Past

From the Tales of Dan Coast

Coast of Christmas Past is the third book in the Dan Coast series of books. Dan Coast is all set to spend Christmas just the same way he has every year for the past few years; alone and drunk. But when uninvited, unexpected guests arrive and throw a wrench into his holiday plans he is forced to sober up (slightly), and throw on a smile. Just when it seems nothing else could go wrong, a close friend is injured in what appears, to the police, to be a drug deal gone bad. Dan Coast and his sidekick, Red jump into action to find the truth while their friend lies unconscious in the hospital.

ISBN: 978-0-9894877-3-3

The Man in Room Number Four

When a mysterious stranger arrives in the small coastal town of Dunquin Cove, Maine it appears as though Claire and her young son, Mica's prayers have been answer.

But who is he, and why is he really here? Join Claire and her guests at the Colsome House Bed and Breakfast as they piece together the mystery of the Man in Room Number Four.

ISBN: 978-0-9894877-2-6

Ship of Fools

From the Tales of Dan Coast

Ship of Fools is the fourth book in The Tales of Dan Coast series and begins where Coasts of Christmas Past left off. Find out how Dan deals with the death of a young friend, while looking into the disappearance of a new friend's sister. Join Dan, Red, and Skip as they fumble their way through a new mystery.

ISBN: 978-0-9894877-4-0

Beach Shoot

A Jake Stellar Series

It's a beautiful Sunday morning in North Myrtle Beach and Emily Bowen, a wife and mother of four, lies dying on the beach. Jake Stellar returns in Beach Shoot, a new mystery by Rodney Riesel.

Beach Shoot is the second Jake Stellar book and sequel to the Amazon Best Seller North Murder Beach. In Beach Shoot, Jake finds himself teamed up with the most unlikely of partners, his nemesis and fellow detective Avis Lint. Join Jake and Avis as they piece together the clues in this thrilling new mystery.

ISBN: 978-0-9894877-5-7